Being with Travis is too tempting.

Ellie walked directly to the tree rack, removed his jacket, and held it out to him. She forced herself to look him squarely in the eyes and smile, refusing to allow him to see how she was quaking inside from her desire to allow all the walls she'd built to fall down and let herself know the joy of his arms once more.

He didn't put the coat on. He crushed it between his hands, his gaze boring into hers. "Thank you."

Sincerity rumbled through the quiet words, weakening the foundation of the distance Ellie was trying to keep.

Travis cupped her cheek gently in one hand, sending tremors through her. "Thank you for tonight, Ellie, for the pictures, for the time with Corey. Thank you for raising our son with such love." The last words were a whisper.

Travis's jacket dropped to the floor. One arm slid about Ellie's waist, pulling her slowly against him. The familiar scent of his Langenfeld cologne enveloped her.

Ellie knew she was going to be in trouble if she didn't stop him, but she couldn't make herself say no. The palms of her hands trembled against his chest. Some traitorous part of her wanted to feel his kiss again, to live in the dream of desire satisfied in loving and trusting this man.

Travis's hand on her cheek tenderly urged her face toward his. His lips touched hers, lightly, testing, warm. Then again, and she leaned into his kiss, welcoming it, remembering it.

It felt so good it was frightening.

JOANN A. GROTE lives in Minnesota where she grew up. She uses the state for most of her story settings, and like her characters, JoAnn seeks to serve Christ in her work. She believes that readers of novels can receive a message of salvation and encouragement from well-crafted fiction. She has had several novels published with Barbour Publishing in the Heartsong Presents line as well as in the American Adventure series for kids.

Books by JoAnn A. Grote

Don't miss out on any of our super romances. Write to us at the following address for information on our newest releases and club information.

Heartsong Presents Readers' Service
PO Box 719
Uhrichsville, OH 44683

Come Home to My Heart

JoAnn A. Grote

Heartsong Presents

To the members of the Forsyth Fellowship of Christian Writers, who believed in my writing before I sold a single manuscript: Margaret Dyson, Martha Green, Debbie Barr Stewart, Allene Robinson, and the late Catherine Jackson. Thank you for your prayers, advice, encouragement, and love.

A note from the author:
I love to hear from my readers! You may correspond with me by writing: **JoAnn A. Grote**
Author Relations
PO Box 719
Uhrichsville, OH 44683

ISBN 1-57748-934-9

COME HOME TO MY HEART

Cover illustration by Adam Wallenta.

PRINTED IN THE U.S.A.

prologue

Ellie Carter reached one red-mittened hand out and slowly lowered the drawer on the mailbox. The cold metal screeched in protest. The December wind spiraled through the Blue Ridge mountain village's short, winding main street, tugging at the brown hair that escaped Ellie's stocking hat. She didn't notice.

Her mittened fingers squeezed more tightly about the square envelope. If she mailed it, it would change her life and her son Corey's life.

She pulled the envelope back and released the drawer. It closed with a bang.

Ellie stared at it unseeing. She trembled all over. She'd spent months building the courage to mail this letter. If she turned away now, would she ever regain the strength to send it?

She grasped the drawer, opened it, and dropped in the envelope. It disappeared silently into the black hole. Her chest felt as though it would split open in fear. *Have I just destroyed my son's life?*

one

I have a son. The thought filled Travis Carter's mind and heart to the exclusion of everyone and everything else.

The sanctuary was fragrant with the scent of pine and burning candles. Organ, trombones, clarinets, and trumpets burst forth in a joyous rendition celebrating the gift of God's Son. The music filled the Los Angeles church with glorious expectation while parishioners waited for the Christmas Eve service to begin.

Travis wasn't thinking of God's Son. His mind was filled with the stunning knowledge that he had a son of his own. He slipped his hand beneath his finely tailored gray suit coat to rest over the monogrammed pocket on his white shirt. He could feel the picture through the cloth. He'd placed the picture there so it would be close to his heart during the service. He wished he could pull it out and stare at it, drink in the image of the laughing two-year-old.

Not that he needed to see the photo to remember what the boy—his son, Corey Travis Carter—looked like: a mass of curly blond hair, blue eyes, pointed chin, a face filled with every two-year-old's joy in discovering something new every day about this experience called life.

The news about Corey had come in an innocent looking envelope that arrived with the usual handful of Christmas cards in the mail. His heart had stopped beating for a moment when he saw his estranged wife's name, Ellie, in the return address. His hands shook as he opened the envelope. Inside was a simple Christmas card, a picture, and a short, to-the-point note from Ellie saying her conscience wouldn't allow her to keep the knowledge of their son from him any longer.

How long had he stood, not moving, staring at that picture?

Disbelief, shock, anger, and finally joy had swept over and through him, leaving him feeling as weak as if he'd swum a mile through heavy surf. When he'd finally roused himself, he'd barely had time to make it to the Christmas service.

As Christmas music swelled about him, questions raced through his mind. Why hadn't Ellie told him about Corey before? She must have been pregnant when they separated, three years earlier. His heart burned at the realization that she may have known she was pregnant when she left. Why had she decided *now* to tell him about Corey? Did she need financial help? She hadn't said anything in the note about child support.

Ellie hadn't said anything about arranging for him to meet the child, either. Had she thought he wouldn't want to meet his own son? Of course he wanted to meet him, get to know him. Would Ellie consider bringing Corey to Los Angeles? Not likely, given how eagerly she'd fled back to the North Carolina mountains when they separated.

Pain ribboned through him as he recalled the days leading up to the separation. He'd been in his first year at the prestigious Los Angeles law firm of Longfellow, Drew, and Prentice, where he still worked, and nervous at attending the company's first Christmas party at the senior partner's home. . . .

№

Travis paused, one hand tight about Ellie's arm, and stared at the brilliantly lit, huge house in front of them. He took a ragged breath. Anticipation was edging out the anger that filled him from the argument he and Ellie had had earlier. "This is it. See you don't do anything to embarrass me."

"I'm sure you can accomplish that without any help from me." She jerked her arm, but he kept his hold on it and started up the walk. He stared straight ahead and could tell she was doing the same.

Travis plastered on a smile when they entered, though it was only a servant who greeted them at the door. Moments later they stood at the edge of the largest living room Travis had ever seen. He counted six overstuffed white sofas and love seats, mixed with antique chairs which looked too uncomfortable for a man to sit upon, arranged in three groupings for easy conversing. Original oil paintings graced the walls. A fire danced and crackled merrily in the fireplace. A Christmas tree which reached the vaulted two-story ceiling glistened with crystal ornaments and perfumed the air with pine scent. A wall of windows, also reaching from floor to ceiling, looked out upon a stone-walled patio. In front of the windows a string quartet played baroque music. Men in tuxedos and women in gowns and jewels mixed laughter and voices with the music.

He heard the sharp intake of Ellie's breath. She touched the fingers of one hand to the base of her throat. "It's beautiful."

It was beautiful. A fierce desire filled him. This home was a symbol of Edward Longfellow's extraordinary success as a lawyer. Travis could see the tall man's head of thick white hair above a group of guests ten feet away. Longfellow glanced in their direction, smiled in recognition, and started toward them.

Travis leaned toward Ellie and said in a low voice from which he couldn't disguise his eagerness, "One day we'll have a place like this."

"Glad you could make it." Edward Longfellow shook Travis's hand, then turned to Ellie. "Good to see you again, Ellie."

It was so like the man to remember Ellie's name, Travis thought, though he'd met her only once before. The partner made it a point to know everything and everyone important to the people important to him. Travis knew he was important to Longfellow, though only because as a member of his firm—even a lowly first-year lawyer—clients and potential clients saw him as a representative of the older man's company.

Travis was glad to see Ellie greeting Longfellow graciously. No hint of the anger between husband and wife remained in her face or in the set of her shoulders.

Mrs. Longfellow, with carefully styled blond hair Travis

suspected was as white as her husband's underneath, slipped up beside them. After greeting them warmly, she stood back and looked Ellie up and down. "My dear, what a lovely gown."

Ellie flushed and darted Travis a short look of triumph. "Thank you."

His anger surged back. He tried to swallow it. It was the dress over which they'd argued earlier. It was long, flowed easily along her slender body. She called the color ice blue. Her dark hair and dark coloring looked good with it, but she'd made it herself. Not that it wasn't beautiful. She was good with a sewing machine, but he'd told her he expected her to wear an expensive gown like the rest of the women would be wearing tonight. She'd refused.

Fury filled his chest to the point of pain. He was sure Mrs. Longfellow was only being kind. Likely tomorrow all the women at the party would be talking about his wife's home-made gown. Not that Ellie had told the woman it was homemade, but a sophisticated woman like Mrs. Longfellow would be sure to know just by looking at it.

He was relieved when Mrs. Longfellow drew Ellie away to introduce her to some other women. He was too angry to be civil to his wife at the moment. He wouldn't want to lose his temper in front of the senior partner.

Travis moved from one group to another, laughing and joking with fellow employees and avoiding Ellie whenever possible. It grew easier to carry on conversation as the night went on and people drank more and more from the partner's generous bar. Travis limited his own drinks to ginger ale or orange juice, and he knew Ellie did the same.

At some point he hooked up with Michelle, another first-year lawyer with the firm. They worked together often. She was smart as a whip and easy-going, fun to work with.

There was only friendship between them, but when Travis looked up and caught Ellie jealously watching Michelle, he decided to show his law associate a little more attention than usual.

It didn't hurt that in addition to being intelligent and funny Michelle was single and had a great figure and long honey-blond hair. She was six inches shorter than he, even in her heels. Between the guests and the music from the string quartet, she had to lean close and lift her head to make him hear her. He was well aware it only made them look more intimate. He smiled to himself, smugly aware of the effect it would have on Ellie. *Serves her right,* he thought, *refusing to dress properly for a party she knows is important to my success at the firm.*

"I'm going to get another drink," Michelle said. "Be back in a minute."

Standing beside the Christmas tree, momentarily alone, Travis stared over the group at Ellie on the other side of the room. She was smiling, but when her gaze met his it grew cold. He knew his own was icy in return.

"Hey, buddy." Don Alexander stepped up beside him, his cheeks only slightly flushed from the effects of liquor. Travis knew Don was always careful of the way he appeared to others. Getting drunk at the boss's party was no way to make an impression and get ahead. Now Don's gaze followed where Travis's had been a moment before. "Not many men watch their own wives at a party. Must say, your wife is something to look at. A real beauty."

Travis grunted what he intended to be taken as agreement. Ellie was a looker all right, with high cheekbones, large brown eyes beneath perfectly shaped dark brows, her face framed with shiny brown hair. If only she hadn't worn that awful gown.

Don cleared his throat and rubbed his hand over his mouth. "You and Michelle are pretty chummy tonight."

He sounded embarrassed, and Travis thought he well should be embarrassed. "We're good friends. You know that."

Don wouldn't meet Travis's gaze. "I'm only going to remind you of this once. I've told you before I think Michelle's interest in you goes beyond friendship or work."

Travis snorted with laughter. "And I said you're wrong."

Don took a deep breath and hiked at his trousers with one hand. "That's what you said all right. See someone over there I need to talk to." He walked away without looking back.

The evening wasn't as much fun after Don's comments. Travis and Ellie left as soon as Travis felt they could do so without appearing overly eager.

The ride home was chilly for a winter night in California, at least in the car. Ellie sat with her arms tight across her chest and stared out at the road, her jaw tight. It was fine with Travis that she hadn't anything to say to him. What could she say? he thought. He was the one who'd been wronged. She knew how important it was to his career that they put forth the right image, and she'd purposely worn that. . .that *thing*.

Back in their apartment—the apartment they couldn't quite afford but which had an impressive-sounding address—they continued their non-verbal argument in the manner familiar to most couples. Both pointedly refused to look at each other or speak, both kept their backs to each other whenever possible, both closed doors with a little more effort than necessary.

Rather than relieving his anger, his refusal to address the issue made the anger build inside Travis. By the time they entered the bedroom, he felt like a red-hot boiler about to burst.

Ellie seated herself on the bench before her vanity and glared into the mirror as she removed the diamond-stud earrings which had been his wedding present to her.

Travis slipped off his jacket and threw it on the bed. "Are you happy now that you wore your stupid dress to the party?"

Ellie silently continued removing her jewelry.

"You can apologize any time for embarrassing me in front of my coworkers and partners," Travis blurted out, hands on his hips.

Ellie's eyebrows lifted. Her gaze met his in the mirror, her brown cyes glittering with a mixture of shock, anger, and pain. "*I* can apologize? If anyone deserves an apology it is me. As for embarrassing you, you managed that all by yourself, trotting around with that woman on your arm all night."

"She wasn't on my arm. Anyway, you could have been beside me. You chose not to be." He looked over her head into the mirror and began loosening his tie.

"You made it obvious you didn't want my company."

His fingers stopped on his tie, but only for a moment. He wasn't about to let her transfer her guilt to himself. "You specifically chose to wear something you knew would embarrass me."

"Did it ever occur to you that as a woman I might know better than you what is appropriate for me to wear?"

He refused to look at her, refused to admit to himself the guilt the pain in her voice shoved toward him.

She swung around on the vanity bench and stood to face him. "I suppose Michelle's off-the-rack dress made it appropriate for you to be seen with her instead of me. Don't you think the colleagues and partners whose good opinion you are always seeking might wonder why you spent the evening with a woman other than your wife?"

"They all know Michelle and I are only coworkers."

"Two of your associates warned me tonight that Michelle is interested in you romantically."

"There's no reasoning with you." Travis grabbed his coat from the bed and headed toward the door.

"Where are you going?"

"I have no idea."

Once in the car Travis drove around aimlessly, his frustration level growing. His intention in spending time with Michelle tonight had been to anger Ellie, not to embarrass himself. Ellie's take on the evening was wrong, he assured himself.

Don's comments about Michelle wriggled into his consciousness. Maybe Ellie was right.

"No!" He slammed an open fist against the steering wheel. He went through all the reasons he was right and Ellie and Don were wrong. When he was done, discomfort still wormed about inside him.

"For a lawyer, I'm a miserable failure at convincing arguments tonight."

It seemed fate when he discovered himself on the street where Michelle lived. He'd dropped her off after work one day when her car was in for repairs. Now he parked in front of the apartment building. If she was home from the party, she most likely hadn't gone to bed yet.

He was right. She was still up. Her voice registered surprise when he announced himself over the security system. Her face registered welcome when he arrived at her door.

She invited him to sit down on the sofa, then she went into the kitchen to get some sodas. Travis slipped off his overcoat and jacket, tossing them over a chair. Relaxing into the overstuffed cream-colored sofa, he undid his cufflinks, set them on a side table, and rolled up his sleeves.

Unease slipped through his chest. Maybe this wasn't such a bright idea, he thought. He shook his head quickly. There was nothing wrong with his being here. He'd tell Michelle about Ellie and Don's accusations, she'd reaffirm how ridiculous the accusations were, and he'd go home with a clean conscience.

"What's up?" Michelle handed him a soda and settled herself on the sofa facing him, her legs drawn up beneath the skirt of her red party dress.

Her easy manner reassured him. He set the soda on the table and leaned back into the cushions, running both hands through his short sand-colored hair. "Ellie and I had a fight tonight. Not a fight exactly, more like an argument. I had to get away for awhile."

Michelle's brows met in concern over large blue eyes. "Do you want to talk about it?"

The sympathy in her manner and soft voice was soothing after the tension between him and Ellie. "Yes." He didn't get any further for a moment. "I don't know where to start."

"Someone once suggested beginning at the beginning."

He gave a short, polite chuckle.

Michelle ran a pink-tipped index finger around the top of

her can. Her gaze followed her finger. "Did it begin before the party or afterward?"

"Before. Mostly before."

She set her can down on the glass coffee table. "Then it didn't have anything to do with me."

Her blunt suggestion caught him off guard. He felt like he'd had all the breath knocked out of him. It was a minute before he could respond. "Why would you think it was about you?"

"I noticed you two didn't spend much time together this evening." She looked down. "And we did." She glanced up suddenly. Her gaze caught his.

He wanted to pull his gaze away but wouldn't let himself. It would be too much like admitting he had done something wrong. He forced a smile and shrugged one shoulder. "I knew you wouldn't take it the wrong way."

She tilted her head, her eyes filled with questions.

"I mean, we work together every day."

"What did you and Ellie argue about?"

Travis hesitated. He'd all but denied Ellie had a problem with him spending so much time with Michelle, yet that was the very thing about which he wanted reassurance. In spite of his confidence in stopping here, he wasn't prepared to be as forthright as Michelle and didn't like the added discomfort of feeling the need to slip sideways into the topic.

"It doesn't matter what it was about. I wanted to get back at her, so I spent more time with you than I probably should have."

"I assume your ploy worked."

"I'll say it did. She's furious. She insists I embarrassed myself and her and you by spending so much time with you that the partners and our colleagues will get the wrong idea."

"The wrong idea would be what?"

He recognized that tone. It sounded a lot like Ellie when he'd put his foot in his mouth. Why did women always want you to put things in black and white? "You know exactly what I mean. Do you think anyone from work would get the impression from the party that we're more than friends and coworkers?" *Anyone besides Don*, he added silently.

"Let's see. First you drop your wife like a hot potato as soon as you arrive. Next you latch onto me for the rest of the evening." She counted the items off on her pink-tipped fingers. "Then you arrive on my doorstep at midnight." She leaned closer. Her shoulder touched his. She looked directly into his eyes. "I don't know about everyone else, but I'm getting the impression you want to be more than friends and coworkers."

Travis's mouth went dry. His mind went blank.

Michelle slipped a hand around his neck. "I don't mind."

He grabbed her shoulder, stopping her before her lips could meet his. "Wait a minute." He stood, holding his hands up, palms toward her. "This isn't what I want."

"Then why are you here?"

He shoved a hand through his hair. "Obviously this was a really dumb move. I'm sorry. Your friendship means a lot to me. I thought you understood."

Michelle crossed her arms. "Do you treat all your friends as weapons against your wife?"

"I'm sorry." He picked up his coat and jacket and backed toward the door.

In the car he leaned his forehead against the steering wheel. "What was I thinking?" In astonishment, he realized he was shaking. Until Michelle made that move on the sofa, he hadn't let himself believe he'd been playing a dangerous game, that he'd been unfair to Michelle as well as to Ellie. He'd come so close to cheating on his wife, something he deplored in others.

He was still shaking when he arrived back at his and Ellie's apartment and lay down on the sofa to sleep.

ॐ

The next morning, Sunday, Travis slept late and woke up stiff. He and Ellie went through the entire day without speaking. It was too humiliating to admit to Ellie that she was right about Michelle's intentions.

He was glad when Monday morning arrived and he could

escape to the office. Delving into preparation for a court case gave his mind welcome relief from his personal problems. He was only assisting a senior partner, but it was an interesting case involving a major movie star's claim against a movie production company for withheld pay.

It was almost eleven when he glanced up from his desk and saw Ellie coming down the hall toward his office with a bounce in her step and a smile on her face. Relief washed away tension he hadn't realized had tightened his shoulders. She'd forgiven him. He could tell by the happy-shy smile on her lips and in her eyes. He was tired of guilt and anger and ready for a reconciliation.

Ellie was almost at his door when Michelle slipped into his office. Travis glanced at her with impatience and opened his mouth to ask her to leave. He never got the words out.

Michelle held a fist toward him. "Here are your cuff links. You left them in my apartment after the party Saturday night."

He barely noticed her triumphant glance before she turned and left the room. His attention was on Ellie, on the stunned look of betrayal in her eyes.

"Is it true?" Ellie asked in a quiet, controlled voice. "Did you go to Michelle's when you left the house Saturday night?"

Travis wished he could deny it honestly. He took a deep breath. "It isn't the way it looks. I went there, yes, but—"

Ellie turned on her heel and started down the hall, her back stiff.

"Ellie!" He hurried after her, all too aware of the other lawyers and clients in the office. Catching up to her, he matched his steps to hers, keeping his voice low, but not managing to keep the desperation from it. "I can explain everything. I promise. I can't leave right now. Longfellow and I are meeting with an important client, but I'll explain everything when I get home tonight."

She left the building without looking at him or saying a word.

Even work couldn't keep his mind from his problems with

Ellie the rest of the day. Longfellow kept him late discussing the case. It was almost eight when he finally arrived at the apartment.

Ellie wasn't there. He sensed it as soon as he walked in, but he didn't begin worrying until he opened the bedroom closet door. He stood grasping the handle, staring in disbelief. All her clothes were gone. All of them, that is, except the ice blue gown.

He found a note from her on the kitchen table, short and to the point. She was returning to her home town in the North Carolina mountains.

In the first anger and pain of her leaving, he didn't go after her. *Good riddance, if that's all the trust she has in me,* he thought. He tore the note in half and flung the pieces to the floor. "She'll be back. I give her a week."

Days slipped into weeks, then months. At first his pride wouldn't let him go after her. Later he reasoned that if she loved him she would return without his asking. There was no point in going after her if she didn't love him, didn't want to be together, was there?

And the months slipped into years.

&

There was a shuffling of feet and pages as the congregation stood for a hymn. Hastily, Travis rose, jerked back to present reality. The Christmas hymn was a familiar one; he didn't need the hymnal, but his throat was too tight from painful memories for the words to get through.

Try as he might to focus on the sermon, his thoughts drifted away to Ellie and Corey in North Carolina. *How could You have let this happen, God?* he raged silently. *How could You have kept me from knowing my son for two whole years? Corey and I will never be able to regain that time. It's lost forever.*

He squeezed his eyes shut. It wasn't God's fault he'd acted like a fool and lost his wife's trust.

It didn't make him feel any better to realize the separation from his son was his own fault.

When he opened his eyes again, his gaze rested on the nativity scene at the front of the church. The pastor's voice barely dented his conscious mind. The baby doll in the manger had captured his attention. He'd never held his son when he was new to this world. The thought gripped his heart and squeezed painfully. Tears pooled in his eyes, blurring the manger and the precious gift it symbolically sheltered.

Had it felt like that to God? Travis sat up straighter, still staring at the manger. Had it felt like that to God, sending His Son to earth? Travis had always heard Christ was thirty-three when He was crucified. The two years Travis had been separated from Corey seemed forever, and Travis had only discovered Corey's existence. How could God have sent His Son to earth, knowing they would be separated for thirty-three years?

Of course, it was a different kind of separation. After all, Jesus was both Son of Man and Son of God. Still, even knowing They would have the rest of eternity together, and that thirty-three years is a short time out of eternity, how could the Father have borne the thought of the separation? *I'm sorry, Lord,* Travis whispered in his mind. It had never before occurred to him to feel sorry for God.

The realization he might never be part of Corey's life dragged Travis's spirits down again. Spending the rest of his life without Ellie wasn't going to be easy, either. He didn't speak of it to others, but he still missed her.

Why had she never sent a separation agreement or divorce papers? Had she been afraid he'd find out about Corey and demand custody?

Travis had never filed for divorce, either. Even before he became a Christian, he'd believed marriage was for keeps. Now he felt guilty every time he read a Bible passage dealing with divorce.

He'd tried to assuage his conscience with the fact that he and Ellie weren't legally divorced. It hadn't worked. He'd wondered whether God wanted him and Ellie to reunite and argued with God against it. It was Ellie who left. He couldn't force her to spend her life with him.

He and Ellie never attended church after their wedding day. He wouldn't want his son brought up not knowing God loved him and would always be there beside him, helping him stand through the tough times that come to everyone. God wouldn't want that, either, would He?

Was it only silly pride that had kept him from trying to win Ellie back? That and the fear of failing, he realized, the risk that she could break his heart all over again. He doubted she'd come back just because he asked her to do so. She thought he was a liar, a cheater. Despair spiraled through him. She didn't trust him, and he hadn't the slightest idea how to go about winning back her trust.

Couldn't the Lord change that? He drew himself up a little straighter in the pew, hope filling his heart. If it was the Lord's will that they be back together, couldn't the Lord show him, dense as he could be about relationships, how to win back her trust?

What if she's found someone else?

He pushed away the voice that whispered in his mind.

The thought of God's separation from Christ returned. Thirty-three years. Travis was only twenty-nine. What if he had to live another twenty-nine years, or thirty-three, or longer without Ellie and Corey?

The congregation rose for the final hymn. As the organ began the introduction to "Joy to the World," Travis lifted a silent prayer. *Please, Lord, restore Ellie to Yourself and me to my family. In the name of the Son You love, amen.*

two

In the back room of her boutique, Ellie Carter carefully stuck in the last pin connecting the finely crafted lace collar to the high neck of the peach linen jacket on the dress form. It was only two weeks after the new year. The boutique was in the middle of its after-Christmas sale, but she'd already completed most of her spring designs.

Ellie darted a glance into the main shop through the workroom door. Brass bells were situated above the boutique door to announce shoppers' arrivals, but she was concerned the bells' music might be drowned out by the *bang, bang, bang* of the carpenter's hammer as he worked on new display shelves.

She lifted the ivory lace gently with one finger. "It's the perfect touch, Anna. My designs wouldn't be the same without your exquisite lace work."

A rose color as gentle as Anna's spirit spread over the woman's wrinkled, soft face. Her faded-blue eyes glowed with pleasure. "I love creating lace. I'd have nowhere to use it if it weren't for you. I'm glad your customers like my lace and your designs."

Ellie fingered the soft linen material and gazed at the simple but sophisticated design. People did seem to appreciate her unique pieces. She hadn't been certain her idea of a boutique made up primarily of her own designs could be successful. She'd been told by a number of owners of more traditional shops that such a shop wasn't possible unless it was in an area which catered to the wealthy, such as Rodeo Drive. This small mountain town was definitely no Rodeo Drive. Still, even though the shop was only three years old, she managed to earn enough to pay the expenses. Barely.

"Travis would never believe it." Instantly she wished she

could catch back the words, though they were true.

"He wouldn't believe people like unique things?"

Ellie unnecessarily straightened the jacket sleeve. "He wouldn't believe I've made a success of this boutique, selling my own designs."

"Why ever not?"

"He's the practical type. Logical. He's a lawyer, remember?"

Anna nodded. "He believes more in statistics than in the power of dreams and inborn ability."

"Yes, that's it exactly." Kinship spread sweet warmth through Ellie. She should have known Anna would understand.

Anna was Ellie's idea of a perfect grandmother, though they weren't related. She was short and petite with sagging jowls, sagging upper arm skin, sagging breasts, and sagging just-about-everything-else except her spirit. Though she worked about her house and yard, she didn't bother trying to keep her body looking twenty-five years younger than its seventy-nine years. She claimed she liked being her age, that each age has its own beauty and excitement, and she couldn't wait to see what the rest of her years held.

Ellie's thoughts drifted back to Travis and the letter she'd mailed three weeks earlier. Why hadn't she heard from him? Turning the form with the peach suit around, she let out a deep sigh.

"What's wrong, dear?" Anna's voice was filled with kind concern.

Ellie hesitated a moment. Anna was always a trusted and wise confidante. In a rush Ellie spilled out the story of the letter. "I thought I'd have heard from him by now, but I haven't."

Anna made a sympathetic sound.

"I don't know whether to be relieved or hurt." Ellie realized she was twisting the peach jacket sleeve in both hands. She dropped it, disgusted with herself. "Is it possible he doesn't even care that he has a son?"

She glanced at Corey, who was sleeping on his back with arms flung out at his sides in complete abandonment in the playpen in the middle of the workroom. Surely if Travis saw Corey he would never be able to leave him.

That thought wasn't comforting.

"Travis may not have received your letter yet. Perhaps he was out of town over the holidays."

"Maybe." Ellie thought a moment. "Some of Travis's law partners used to spend the Christmas and New Year holidays at Aspen."

"Even if he's received the letter, it must be quite a shock to suddenly find oneself a father. You said you weren't sure whether you should have sent the letter," Anna reminded Ellie gently. "Will you be relieved if you don't hear from Travis?"

"I don't know." Ellie plopped inelegantly onto a scruffy bentwood chair, situated where she could keep an eye on the shop. "I argued with the Lord for months over whether to tell Travis about Corey. Every negative thought plagued me. What if Travis wants custody, and is granted it? It would be like tearing out my heart to lose Corey."

Anna lowered herself to the oak stool beside Ellie. "I know, dear. No use pretending it might not come to that, but I'm sure at the worst the judge would only award Travis partial custody."

"Maybe." Ellie wasn't convinced. She'd heard of too many decisions by judges in child custody cases that made no sense to her at all.

"Would you trust Travis to raise Corey?"

Ellie's gaze moved again to her son. She felt her face soften. He looked so much like his father with the blond hair and blue eyes. "I don't know. When I met Travis in college I thought he was the most wonderful man in the world. He wanted to fight for people who need justice."

"He sounds like a good man."

"Mmmm. We married right after graduation. Then he entered law school. He did brilliantly and his instructors predicted a great future for him." She shook her head. "He interned with a major law firm. Soon he was more in love with the idea of becoming a big-bucks lawyer than with the ideals of justice."

Anna shook her head, making a "tch, tch, tch" sound.

"The scariest thing," Ellie continued, "is that Travis doesn't believe in God. I hate to think of Corey being raised by someone who doesn't love Christ."

Ellie hadn't believed in God either when she left Travis. Out on her own for the first time in her life with a baby on the way, she discovered she needed a firm foundation on which to build her and her baby's lives. She'd sought help in church and eventually came to believe in Christ. Now He was like a close friend. *I would never have made it without Him.*

Anna sat quietly, apparently turning over in her mind everything Ellie had said. The banging of the carpenter's hammer continued while Ellie waited. When Anna spoke, her tone was sincere. "You decided it was right to tell him of Corey in spite of those fears?"

"Yes. I couldn't erase the conviction that Travis has a right to know his own son. Believe me, I tried for years to erase it. I kept hoping for a sign from God, assurance that everything would work out in a way I could easily accept."

"You didn't get an answer like that."

"No." Ellie could tell from Anna's tone that she'd learned through her long life such easy answers are rare. "The only answer I received was that God loves Corey and wants the best for him more than I do." She turned to Anna. "I've learned to trust the Lord in so many ways in my life during the last three years. Trusting Him with Corey is more difficult than anything I've ever had to do."

One of Anna's soft, wrinkled hands patted Ellie's. Anna's smile was filled with a joy and peace that made her eyes sparkle. "It's a great blessing to our Father when we trust Him with the things we love the most."

Ellie darted Anna a look of surprise. "I never thought of anything we do as blessing Him." Her gaze swivelled back to sleeping Corey. He looked so innocent, so. . .vulnerable. A sudden lump of pain filled her throat. "What do parents do who believe God will protect their children, and yet awful things happen to their sons and daughters? How do they ever reconcile that with a loving Father God? How would I?"

"That is the hardest test of our faith, when painful things happen to our children." Anna's voice had dropped to such a soft level that Ellie instinctively leaned forward to hear her better. "We're tempted to forget at such times that the children don't really belong to us at all. They belong to God, the same as we do. I believe each child has his own mission on this earth, a mission that doesn't always coincide with what we with our limited sight believe is right for that child." She was silent a moment. "It's the only way I've been able to keep my faith through some things."

The last sentence hung in the air with an emotional force Ellie seldom felt. Her chest tightened in compassion. Anna had lost a grandchild to leukemia. A difficult way to learn the lesson she'd just shared. It was a lesson Ellie had no wish to learn from experience.

The carpenter stopped in the workroom doorway. "You want to see what I've done so far?" He jerked his head back over his shoulder toward the shop.

"Sure, Chuck." Ellie stood up.

Corey let out a tentative cry, a typical I'm-awake-is-anyone-going-to-pick-me-up cry. Ellie laughed. "I guess the quiet after your hammering woke him." She gave Chuck a teasing grin.

Anna shooed Ellie away with a wave of her hand. "I'll take care of Corey. You go check out Chuck's work. Have to keep an eye on that young man, you know." Anna chuckled at her own joke.

Chuck looked down from his six feet to Ellie's five-foot-five and grinned. "Does she mean me or Corey?"

Ellie laughed. "Both of you, probably."

Chuck stopped beside the shelves on which he'd been pounding for what seemed hours to Ellie. "What do you think? Do they blend with your cabinets all right?"

"They're perfect." They were. Chuck had gone to a lot of trouble to match the new shelves to the antique cabinet she had bought last month. He'd stained the wood to match as closely as possible, aging it in some way mysterious to Ellie. Unable to locate molding to match, he'd carved it himself. Ellie ran a hand lightly over the side of the cabinet. "You put so much of yourself into your work. No wonder everything you make is wonderful."

His already straight shoulders straightened slightly more in pride and pleasure. "Wouldn't go to all this trouble for just anyone."

"Yes, you would. You're an artist with wood."

His posture relaxed a little. His gaze traveled over the cabinet. "It feels that way sometimes."

Ellie breathed a soft sigh of relief. She'd successfully turned his comments to his work. Perhaps she was misjudging him. Perhaps he hadn't meant that he had gone to all the trouble with the cabinet because she was more than a friend or client. All too often, however, his normal friendliness had taken on more intimate tones. Nothing out-and-out romantic, but too close for comfort.

She opened the doors of the antique cabinet she was using to display sweaters which had been knit by a local woman and trimmed in Anna's crocheted lace. "Could you check the hinge on this door, Chuck? It's loose, just a smidgin."

"Best time to catch it." He moved close behind her, reaching both arms to check the top hinge.

Ellie slipped from between him and the cabinet door and watched him work.

He was so different from Travis. About the same height, but built slighter. Not skinny. The muscles in his forearms reminded her of taut rubber bands. His hair was straight and dark brown beneath one of the baseball hats he always wore. Travis's hair was curly and blond, and he wouldn't be caught dead in a baseball hat. Just the thought of him in one made her smile.

Chuck turned to reach for a screwdriver from his small red tool chest and caught the smile. "What's the joke?"

"Nothing."

He brushed unnecessarily at the front of his long-sleeved gray T-shirt. "Did I get something on me?"

"No. I was just thinking of a funny memory."

"I can always use a laugh."

"It's the kind of thing that doesn't translate well."

Chuck shrugged, turned back to the cabinet, and began removing screws in the lower hinge. "You and Corey have plans for dinner?"

She didn't answer immediately. Often during the last three years she'd shared meals with him without giving it a second thought. His calm wisdom had always been available when she needed a friend. But now. . .

"I won tickets for two free meals at the Black Bear Café's New Year's drawing. Thought maybe you'd help me use them."

It sounded innocent enough. "Thanks. It will be nice for both Corey and me to get out for a little while."

Maybe she was building a mountain out of the proverbial mole hill. Maybe he wasn't showing undue interest in her. Maybe she was tired of being alone and wanted to believe a man was romantically interested in her. She caught back a groan. A romantic interest was a complication and temptation she didn't need in her life.

The brass bells tinkled, announcing a customer. Ellie swung about, her usual welcoming smile in place.

It froze. All of her froze.

"Travis."

three

Ellie's thoughts tumbled about like sticks in rapids. She'd thought he would write or call, not travel across the country without letting her know he was coming.

"Hello, Ellie."

"Hi." The word sounded as breathless as she felt.

Hands in the pockets of his gray wool jacket, he glanced about the shop. "Nice place."

Her fears rushed back full force. *Why is he here? Does he think by arriving unexpectedly he can gain an advantage? He's a lawyer. He must know all kinds of legal tricks to help him gain custody of Corey.*

Chuck moved close behind Ellie. "You here on business, mister?"

Ellie could hear the threat in his calm, even voice. She was grateful for his support, even though she didn't need his protection. "This is my hus. . .this is Travis. Travis Carter, Chuck Beckett."

The men exchanged curt nods. Neither one offered his hand. Ellie felt Chuck tense. "It's all right," she reassured him.

Chuck took a step, slapping the screwdriver lightly against an open palm. "I'll be in the back room if you need me."

She nodded. Neither she nor Travis spoke until Chuck reached the workroom.

"He acts like I'm a serial killer." Travis's voice was low in an obvious attempt to keep from being overheard. It carried a rumble of anger. "What have you been telling people about me?"

She began straightening the sweaters inside the cabinet, not wanting to face him. "I don't spread my personal life around as though it's everyone's business."

A moment of silence. "I'm sorry. I guess I jumped to a

conclusion. I didn't mean for us to start out this way. It's just
. . .a little uncomfortable."

How could it not be uncomfortable? Ellie stared unseeing
at her hands resting on a rose sweater. She took a deep breath
and turned to face him. "You must have received my card."

He nodded once, briskly. "And the picture."

Silence again. It strained Ellie's muscles, as if she were trying to bring a wild bronco at the end of a rope under control.
Travis's unspoken accusations hurled themselves through her
brain: *Why didn't you tell me earlier that I had a son? How
could you leave me knowing you were carrying our child?*

"I want to meet him, Ellie." Determination underlined the
simple, quiet words.

"Of course." She wondered that her voice didn't tremble
the way her heart was trembling. She'd known when she
mailed the card that if he chose to see Corey she wouldn't
fight it. Still, the reality frightened her.

Travis let out a sigh of relief, and she realized he had actually thought she might say no. *Why, he's afraid, too!* The
knowledge calmed her somewhat.

"Tonight?" he asked.

"I. . .I have dinner plans."

"When, then? I'd like to meet him as soon as possible."

Ellie ran the palms of her hands down the sides of her
skirt, then caught her fingers together in front of her to end
their betrayal of her nervousness. She should tell him Corey
was in the back room. They could meet now. But she wasn't
ready yet. Tonight or tomorrow was too soon, even though
she'd set the meeting in motion by letting him know of
Corey's existence.

It was too late to turn back. She'd cancel her plans with
Chuck. "Tonight, after dinner, if that suits you."

"That's fine." Travis's shoulders dropped a couple inches.

"It will have to be early. I usually put Corey to bed about
eight. Could you be at my place about seven?"

"I'll be there. Are you still staying with your folks?"

"They spend winters in Florida now that they're retired. I have a place of my own." She gave him directions. As soon as they were out of her mouth, she regretted her decision. Perhaps it would have been wiser to meet him on neutral ground, not to let him know where she lived. She dismissed the thought. It was a small town. If he wanted to know her address, he could find it out with little trouble.

"I'll see you at seven." The brass bells tinkled merrily above his stiff back when he walked out.

She shivered. The chill winter air his leaving let in bit at her body as his arrival had bitten at her spirit.

❧

Travis went quickly up the wooden front steps of the old two-story frame house. It was a modest place, but so were most homes in the small mountain village. A porch, its floor slightly slanting from age, crossed the front of the building. Lace curtains at the large windows discreetly and daintily allowed a sense of privacy. The front door, which he guessed was original to the house, had a large oval etched window.

Travis frowned. A door like that wasn't safe. Anyone could break in without half trying. He pushed away the thought, reminding himself this wasn't Los Angeles.

He became aware of the tension in his shoulders. He took a moment to breathe deeply, then roll his head to loosen the muscles in his neck. He snorted in disgust. He hadn't been this tense since his first appearance as a lawyer before the bar.

He admired the workmanship of the beautiful window while he knocked. He could see through the lace-covered window that it wasn't Ellie who was answering. The door was opened by a slender blond woman about his own age, wearing tight jeans and a cropped red top.

"I'm sorry. I thought Ellie Carter lived here." He took a step backward, his glance darting to the tarnished brass numbers beside the door.

"She does. You must be Travis."

At his nod, the woman opened the door wider. "Come in.

I'm Jessica. My son, Brent, and I share the house with Ellie and Corey." She reached out a hand, and an armful of silver bracelets jangled.

Travis shook her hand.

Jessica pointed to the large stuffed gray horse with a white mane and tail tucked under one of Travis's arms. "Good choice."

His cheeks heated. "Thanks." He'd wanted to buy the whole toy store for Corey. A stuffed animal seemed like a mundane first gift for his son, but in the toy store he'd faced the sobering fact that he didn't know what toys Corey had or what kind he liked.

He'd barely entered the house when a wailing call came from the second floor. "Mo-o-o-m!"

Travis's heart lurched at the toddler's voice. Was that his son?

Jessica groaned and rolled her eyes, then grinned. "That's my son."

Travis's chest deflated.

"Make yourself comfortable in the living room. Ellie will be down in a minute." She hurried up the open staircase that bordered the hall, climbing over a gate at the top. Travis recognized it as a child safety device.

Jessica was a surprise. Travis was relieved to find Ellie wasn't sharing the house with a man. If she was seeing someone, she must not have made a commitment to him yet.

Travis walked slowly into what was obviously the living room. The room opened directly onto the hall by an open wall. Tall, brightly polished wooden columns stood on each side of the opening.

The room was high ceilinged with thick dark woodwork in the tradition of the early 1900s. The furniture looked like it came from the same period. The navy blue overstuffed sofa and chairs were worn until the cushions were almost bare, yet they looked comfortable and welcoming. Dark wooden tables with intricate carvings were similarly worn.

The difference between this shabby room and the smart

apartment he and Ellie had shared in Los Angeles made him shiver.

He set the horse behind one of the chairs where Corey wouldn't see it as soon as he entered the room.

Making his way toward the old-fashioned piano with a display of pictures covering the top, he stumbled. "What. . .?" A yellow and black plastic dump truck rolled slowly across the faded, rose-covered beige rug, propelled by the energy of his errant foot.

A glance about showed it wasn't the only toy. Other plastic trucks and autos in bright reds, blues, and yellows were scattered about the floor. A Nerf ball so orange he wondered if it glowed in the dark rested beneath the piano bench. A pale brown teddy bear with a well-loved look reclined upside down on the sofa. Was the bear Corey's or Brent's? Would Corey prefer it to the horse?

Unexpected joy curled through Travis. Some of these were his son's toys. Travis crouched down, balancing himself on the fronts of his shoes, and pushed the dump truck around one of the piano bench legs before winding up the box on the back of the truck. The hours he'd spent playing with a dump truck just like this when he was a boy came back in a rush.

"Don't drive too fast. You wouldn't want to get a speeding ticket."

At Ellie's voice, Travis jerked his head up so fast he fell back on his bum. Ellie's smirk turned into a laugh.

Travis's neck and face heated, and he grinned sheepishly. "Just remembering when I was a kid." He got to his feet. "Where's Corey?"

"Jessica will bring him down in a minute. She thought we might want to say hello first." Ellie swung her weight from one foot to the other, her long brown skirt swinging gracefully. Her eyes seemed to look everywhere except at him.

We're like two cats trying to decide whether to be friends or attack each other, Travis thought.

"Can I take your coat?"

He handed it to her, noticing the wedding band on her left hand. Surprise danced through him at the encouraging sign. Why had she removed the solitaire diamond engagement ring and left the wedding ring?

He glanced about the room. There were no mementos from their life together. No wedding picture on the wall. Why should he have thought there would be? Their wedding photo still hung on the wall of the California apartment, right where she'd hung it the day they moved in. She'd left the wedding album, too, he remembered, trying to ignore the pang that shot through him.

When she returned from the hall closet, Travis searched his mind for something neutral to say, anything but what he wanted to say, anything but the questions that had built up inside him since he'd received her card on Christmas Eve. "How old is Brent?"

"Three and a half, a year older than Corey. They're best buddies."

"That's good. That he has a friend near his own age, I mean."

"Yes." Ellie's gaze again searched the room.

The sound of footsteps and boyish voices came from the stairway. Ellie turned toward it. "Here they come." Travis thought from her face that she looked relieved, but her shoulders appeared tense, riding a bit higher than normal beneath her burgundy-colored sweater.

Then he noticed his own shoulders were tense, and he realized he was watching Ellie to avoid looking at Corey. He hadn't expected this wonderful moment to be ribboned through with fear. Maybe fear wasn't the right word, but he knew his life would never be the same once he looked on the face of his son.

Travis turned his head slowly. There was one boy on either side of Jessica, one brunet and one blond, each clutching one of her hands. They leaped bravely down one step after another as though descending the stairway were an exciting adventure. Travis recognized Corey immediately. The blond curls and laughing blue eyes were the same as those in the picture Travis had carried with him since the day it arrived at his apartment.

He rubbed a hand over his mouth, trembling with the effort to stay where he was and not rush across the room and wrap the boy in his arms. To do so would only frighten Corey.

Ellie held out a hand to him. "Come and meet your. . .our friend, Travis."

Travis glanced at her face. It was noticeably paler than a minute earlier. It hadn't occurred to him that she wouldn't introduce him to Corey as his father. Of course, it was only sensible that she didn't push it on the child right away. Still, he hadn't been prepared for how much it would hurt to be introduced as anything less than Corey's father, how much it would hurt not to be able to acknowledge their relationship. He wished he and Ellie had discussed this before Corey came downstairs. How many other things should they have resolved before he met Corey?

The boy hurried to Ellie, smiling. Even that simple act cut through Travis's heart. Would his son ever come to him in that trusting manner?

Corey leaned against Ellie's leg. Curiosity filled his face as he looked Travis over. He held up a hand, fingers splayed. "Hi."

"Hi, Corey." Travis mirrored the boy's gesture, then stuffed his hands in the pockets of his khakis. He smiled at Corey, meeting the boy's curious gaze, waiting patiently while Corey studied him.

"You've met Jessica," Ellie said. "This is her son, Brent."

Travis tore his gaze from his son to glance at the other woman and boy. Travis lifted his palm again. "Hi, Brent. Nice to meet you."

"Hi." The word was muffled as Brent burrowed his head into his mother's thigh, while trying to keep one eye on Travis.

Jessica smoothed Brent's long brown hair with one hand. "We're going out to eat," she explained to Travis, pulling on a jacket. "We won't be late."

Jessica hesitated at the door, looking at Ellie uncertainly. Travis had the uncomfortable feeling Jess was afraid to leave Ellie and Corey alone with him.

He was glad when the front door shut behind them. He studied Ellie's face. Surely she wasn't afraid of him. Her wide brown eyes and broad face did seem tense, though. Likely she felt as uncomfortable and uncertain as he did about this evening.

Corey hurried across the room with his wide-legged two-and-a-half-year-old's gait. His eyes sparkled when he picked up the dump truck. He held it up for Travis to see. A grin dotted with baby teeth spread across his face. "Mine."

Travis dropped to one knee. "That's a great truck."

"Look." Corey squatted down and turned the handle that lifted the dump truck.

"Wow. That's pretty terrific."

Corey grunted agreement and concentrated on winding the dump truck back down. "See?"

"I sure do."

Corey searched the floor with his gaze, then pounced on a tiny stuffed dog. He dropped it into the truck. "Look," he demanded again. Once more he twisted up the back of the truck, then opened the back and let the dog slip out. His mission a success, he dropped back his head and beamed up at Travis, awaiting praise.

"Good job. Do you haul things besides dogs in your dump truck?"

Corey nodded and looked for another load.

Travis was amazed at the joy that filled him watching his son perform these simple acts. How was it possible he hadn't known Corey existed, even without being told? Travis couldn't take his gaze from the boy, couldn't bear a moment in Corey's presence without watching him.

It was obvious Corey enjoyed having such a rapt audience. He pulled toy after toy from the wooden box with the hinged top beneath a window, showing each toy to Travis, who dutifully exclaimed over it and asked how it worked. As each toy was discarded for the next, Ellie tried re-placing it in the box. Sometimes she actually managed to put a toy away without Corey catching sight of her and issuing a loud and demanding "No!"

Ellie ignored the command the sixth time and put a plastic tool bench back in the box.

Corey rushed over to recover it, his face red with fury. "No!"

"We put our toys away when we're done, remember?" Ellie reminded gently.

Corey didn't answer. He retrieved the tool bench, sat down on it, and went back to showing off his large red fire engine.

Travis roared with laughter.

Ellie's hands landed on her hips. "Don't encourage him."

"He wants to show me his toys. What's the harm in that?"

"He wants to have his own way, you mean. I don't need anyone encouraging him to disobey me."

"You're right. I'm sorry." Travis couldn't help smiling. He and Ellie sounded like any two parents.

Travis thought it all too soon when Ellie announced Corey's bedtime. Corey thought it was too soon, too. He sat among his toys, refusing to look at her, and repeated his favorite word. "No."

Ellie wasn't about to be deterred. She picked up the worn teddy bear from the couch. "Here's Teddy. Say goodnight to Travis and we'll take Teddy upstairs to bed."

Corey shook his head until his curls bounced. His bottom lip stuck out in a pout, and he concentrated harder on the toy in his hands.

Travis gave it a try. "If you go to bed with your mother, I'll give you a present."

Corey's head lifted. His eyes brightened.

"Travis." Ellie's one word was a protest.

Travis took the stuffed horse from behind the chair, knelt down, and held it out. "Here you go, partner."

Corey's face lit up. "A pony!" He couldn't get to it fast

enough. The rest of his toys were instantly forgotten. He held it tightly, brushing the mane and tail with one hand.

"What do you say to Travis?" Ellie reminded.

"Thank you." Corey was too busy studying the horse's face to look up.

Corey's obvious pleasure was nothing compared to Travis's joy that his gift was so well received. "What will you name the pony?"

"Pony," was the instant and decisive answer.

"Very appropriate." Travis exchanged an amused glance with Ellie.

Ellie held out a hand to Corey. "Say goodnight to Travis."

Corey ignored her, devoting his attention to the horse.

"Pony hasn't seen your bedroom yet. Don't you want to show it to him?" she suggested.

Corey appeared to consider this. "Okay." He struggled to his feet, the large horse hindering his progress. " 'Night T'avis."

" 'Night, so. . .Corey."

"Do you want to give Travis a hug?"

Travis could have hugged Ellie for suggesting it, even though he detected a strain in her voice.

Corey shook his head and leaned against Ellie's leg, eyeing Travis warily.

His lack of trust lacerated Travis's heart, but he forced a smile. "That's all right, partner. No one should hug anyone they don't want to hug. I'll be glad to be your friend anyway."

"I'm sorry," Ellie mouthed.

"Any chance I could help put him to bed?"

"No." She blurted the word. "It will only take longer to settle him down if you do." The excuse sounded lame to Travis, but he hadn't any choice but to accept her decision. He watched the two until they reached the top of the stairs and were lost to his sight.

A minute later Jessica and Brent returned. After a few brief words they also went upstairs. Travis could hear the women talking.

Travis picked up the toys scattered about the floor and put them back in the toy box. He plopped down on the sofa and poked an index finger into the worn teddy bear's stomach, fiercely glad his son had chosen the pony over this old favorite.

I love that boy, he thought. He'd loved him from the first time he read about him in Ellie's note on Christmas Eve. His own son, the only person on earth who was literally a part of him. Travis had heard a father's love could be like that, instant and complete, but he hadn't believed it. He'd seen too many cases in his law practice where blood ties apparently meant nothing.

"I only want the best for you, Corey." Travis rested his head against the sofa, reliving the time spent with Corey, watching his eyes shine with fun and excitement, listening to his wonderful little-boy laugh, sharing the joy of him with Ellie. If he and Ellie got back together, they could spend every evening like that, like a real family.

The vision caught at his heart, both in hope and in pain at the fear it might never happen. *God is in control,* he reminded himself. *He will work everything together for good.*

He tried not to dwell on the fact that the separation was his own fault, the result of his own foolish actions. Flirting with Michelle had been the most unwise choice of his life. He shifted uneasily. Would one of the consequences of his flirting be a lifetime separated from Ellie and their son?

When Ellie returned he immediately sat up straight. He caught her amused look, realized he was hugging the teddy bear to his chest, and hastily tossed it back onto the couch.

She walked across the room slowly with her hands caught behind her back. "Your horse was a big success."

"I'm glad."

Ellie sat on the edge of the cushion on the other end of the sofa. "We have some things to discuss."

Travis agreed. He was aware of the boundaries between himself and Ellie, boundaries he wasn't willing to test or cross over. He could sense Ellie's defenses were up. He began with a simple question. "When is Corey's birthday?"

It was his unspoken questions he most wanted to ask. Was she afraid he might try to take Corey away from her? What would she think if she knew he'd been entertaining the thought of the three of them together as a family? If that didn't happen, he couldn't promise he wouldn't try to gain custody if he decided it was in Corey's best interest. The connection he'd seen between Ellie and Corey tonight looked healthy. Travis wished everything could be resolved immediately, but he knew it would take time for him and Ellie to know what they each wanted, and what each of them could give in the situation.

"Corey seems happy. You must be a good mother."

She slipped her hands about one knee, looking instantly more relaxed. "Thank you."

"Do you need financial help?"

Ellie bristled visibly. "My boutique hasn't made me wealthy, but I manage to support Corey and myself."

Travis felt like he was interviewing a hostile client, trying to lessen Ellie's tension with conciliatory and non-threatening comments and actions. "I'm sure you do, but it's my responsibility as much as yours to support Corey. How about if I give you a check each month?" He suggested an amount.

Ellie hesitated. "Shouldn't that be determined by the courts or something?"

He started sweating. He hoped things would never come to a divorce or custody hearing. "I'll give you whatever amount you think is fair. The courts can change it later if they wish." He might advise against this if he were his client.

She agreed to his offered amount. "I'll put it in a savings account for him." She glanced down at her hands. "I. . .I owe you an apology. I should have told you about Corey earlier. You have every right to be angry with me."

"I was at first. Now all I want is for us both to put away blame and anger and get on with our lives. I only want to know my son, to be part of his life."

Ellie's gaze met his. "How do we do that?" she asked quietly.

He shrugged. "I guess we figure it out as we go."

The silence between them grew long, and the longer it grew the thicker with tension the air became.

He swallowed hard, his heart speeding up as he considered the question burning his tongue. "Did you know you were pregnant with Corey when. . ." He searched for a phrase that wouldn't sound accusatory, "when you came back here to your home town?"

Ellie's face became mask-like. Her arms folded over her chest, her hands clutched her upper arms. "I found out the morning I left. I went directly to your office from the doctor's office to share the news with you." Her voice was as emotionless as her face.

Travis stared at her in shock, remembering the joy on her face when she came to his office that morning. He'd thought she'd merely forgiven him. Pain charged through Travis's chest like a lightning bolt. If he hadn't acted the fool with Michelle, he wouldn't have been separated from Ellie and Corey all this time, wouldn't be sitting here now afraid he might be separated from them for the rest of his life. If only he could make her understand. "About Michelle—"

"I don't want to hear it." Her angry words cut through his attempt.

"But it wasn't what you think."

"I said I don't want to hear it." Ellie shot to her feet, her brown eyes flashing. "It's in the past."

"All right." He rose to face her. *If we can't discuss it, how can there be forgiveness and healing for us, and without healing, how can it ever be in the past?* he wondered.

Ellie crossed her arms tightly over her chest. She rocked slightly back and forth. "What do you plan to do now?"

About Corey. The unspoken words shouted in the air between them.

Suddenly Travis knew exactly what he was going to do. "I don't want Corey to grow up not knowing his father, not knowing me. I'm moving here as soon as possible."

four

Ellie and Jessica left Corey and Brent playing in the church nursery and walked together into the sanctuary, greeting friends on their way to the pew where they always sat with Anna.

Ellie glanced about with a puzzled frown as they took their seats. "I wonder where Anna is? She's usually here by now."

"I hope she isn't ill." Jessica paged through the hymnal locating the first song. "We know last night's snowstorm didn't keep her away." Anna lived two houses from the stone church, so even inclement weather never kept her away in spite of her seventy-nine years.

"Let's stop and check on her on the way home."

Jessica nodded agreement. Then her face brightened. "Here she is."

Ellie turned toward the aisle. Her smile froze. Anna was coming toward them on Travis's arm, looking positively delighted with the attention the two of them were drawing from the curious congregation.

Anna's eyes sparkled as she and Travis stopped beside the pew. Ellie wouldn't have said Travis's eyes sparkled, but he looked pleased at her surprise.

"There isn't room for both of us in your pew," Anna whispered loudly. "We'll just sit in this one." She indicated the pew in front of them.

"What is he doing here?" Ellie mouthed to Jessica.

Jessica shrugged and sent her a look of pity, then stood with the rest of the congregation as the opening strains of the first hymn swelled through the church.

Ellie belatedly followed.

She tried to keep her mind on the service. It wasn't easy

with her estranged husband seated directly in front of her. What was he doing at the service? She hadn't seen him in a church since their marriage ceremony. In college they'd had many long discussions about what they believed, or rather did not believe, about God. Travis always said he didn't know and didn't care whether there was a God. "If there is," he had said more than once, "He can mind His business and I'll mind mine and we'll get along just fine."

Perhaps Anna had invited him, Ellie speculated, and he'd thought it rude to refuse. He was living in Anna's home, after all, renting her upstairs apartment. He'd moved in two days ago, just over a month after he announced in Ellie's living room his intention to move to town.

Ellie could hardly believe Travis had given up his position with the prestigious law firm to live in this small mountain village to be closer to Corey. She knew he was planning to practice law here but didn't know any details about his business plans.

Likely he'll soon tire of our village, she thought. He probably hadn't quit the Los Angeles law firm, merely taken a leave of absence and sublet the apartment. Maybe he was only here to win over Corey and determine the best way to gain custody.

That's not fair. Perhaps it wasn't, but this small-town, church-going lawyer certainly wasn't the man she'd left three years ago. So who was the real Travis Carter now?

She wished he wasn't sitting right in front of her. In spite of distrusting his motives, an old familiar longing stirred in her. The shape of his head and shoulders, the way he moved, his hair: all brought back memories of the time she'd loved him completely, memories of laughter, of struggling together, of loving together, intimate memories she'd been trying to forget for three years.

Memories from when she'd been innocent and naive, when she'd trusted him with every inch of her heart and being.

The harshness of broken trust mixed with desire for the time before disillusionment had changed her life forever. She hated the painful way the conflicting emotions twisted inside her.

Had she been wrong to tell Travis about Corey? she wondered for what seemed the thousandth time. *Lord, I need Your guidance now more than ever.*

During the last three years, she'd relied on the Lord's guidance constantly. Everything had been new and frightening: being a first-time mother and the only support for herself and Corey, finding a place to live, beginning her own business. Everywhere she'd turned stood unfamiliar challenges to face. Struggling to learn to hear the Lord's voice, she'd come across Colossians 3:15 in her Amplified Bible. "And let the peace (soul harmony which comes) from the Christ rule (act as umpire continually) in your hearts—deciding and settling with finality all questions that arise in your minds."

Now, when she needed guidance desperately, she kept concentrating on her fears and couldn't feel peace. She'd dealt with fears before, but this time she couldn't seem to get past them.

When the service was over, Travis turned around with that broad smile Ellie loved and distrusted at the same time. "Hi. Where's Corey?"

"In the nursery."

"Do you attend here often?"

"Every Sunday." Ellie could hear Jessica and Anna chatting beside them. "I'm surprised to see you here."

"I could say the same."

Ellie placed the hymnal in its holder on the back of the pew. "I've changed. I'm not the person you knew."

"Me, either."

"Really?"

He ignored her sarcastic tone. "I'm glad you're raising Corey in the church."

His statement shocked her so that she couldn't think of a reply. She was glad when Anna turned to them with an invitation. "I've a roast in the oven. Won't you and Corey join Travis and me for dinner? Jessica has already agreed to come."

Ellie hesitated. All she wanted was to take Corey home and get away from Travis's disturbing presence, but Anna loved to have company and she was such a dear. "Of course. It's lovely of you to ask us."

Anna beamed. "I love doing for folks. I'm so glad Travis moved into my apartment. It's nice having company for meals again. The last tenants kept to themselves."

"You're cooking for Travis?" Ellie directed the question to Anna but her disapproving gaze fixed on Travis.

He spread his hands in a how-could-I-say-no-to-the-sweet-lady gesture, but his smile told her he was pleased with the arrangement. "Anna is a great cook."

His charm obviously worked on Anna, who couldn't have looked more pleased. Ellie remembered how well his easy charm had worked on her during most of their relationship. She determined to steel herself against it in the future, for her own sake and for Corey's.

Anna introduced Travis to Pastor Evanson at the church door. "He just moved here."

Pastor Evanson invited him to join the men's weekly prayer breakfast.

"I'd like that. Where and when?"

"The Black Bear Café, Wednesday mornings at six-thirty."

"I'll be there."

Ellie eyed Travis with suspicion. Travis at a prayer breakfast? She couldn't imagine it. What was behind this apparent change of heart? Did he think becoming involved in the church was a good way to meet potential clients?

Ellie had to agree with Travis on Anna's baking talents as they finished up her coconut cake dessert a couple hours later. The meal had been more pleasant than Ellie expected. Travis kept them all entertained with stories of a lawyer's life in L.A., which could easily have been the basis for a television program titled *Funniest Courtroom Videos*.

Corey and Brent had tired of the dinner table. They were

arguing over a stuffed dog on wheels in the living room. Ellie kept an eye on them, hoping the argument would stay mild, while Anna served coffee in delicate porcelain cups.

"Isn't it difficult to start a law practice from scratch with no clients?" Anna asked Travis when she sat down.

Ellie was glad Anna had asked the question. She'd wondered the same but hadn't wanted to show an interest in Travis's life by asking.

He took his gaze from the boys reluctantly to answer Anna. It seemed Travis hadn't stopped watching Corey since they arrived. Ellie hated to admit it, but Travis's apparent fascination with their son was so touching it made her chest glow with warmth. She was sure he'd rather be on the floor playing with the boys now than drinking coffee from fragile cups with three women. She took a sip, repressing a giggle.

Travis rested his elbows on the table. "It is hard starting from scratch. With that in mind, I spoke with a large regional firm in Charlotte. I'd met one of the partners on a ski trip last winter. I suggested opening a branch office here, with me as the firm's representative. He and his partners agreed to give it a try. That way I don't carry all the financial risk myself, and the firm's name, which is well known in the Carolinas, will draw some clients."

"Where will you work?" Ellie asked.

"I've arranged to rent the downstairs of the vacant Brandy-wine building for an office. It needs remodeling to meet our needs, of course. I've talked with your friend Chuck, Ellie. He's agreed to start working on it next week."

"That's wonderful." Anna smiled at him over the brim of her cup.

Ellie didn't think it was at all wonderful. Wonderful would be if Travis had stayed in L.A. and been content to send Corey birthday and Christmas presents.

Her conscience tweaked. She did want Corey to have a regular father, one who would be there for him through good times and hard times and growing times, but was Travis capable of being a responsible father?

Corey threw himself against her thigh. She barely managed to keep her coffee from sloshing over the rim onto Anna's antique lace tablecloth. "Whoa! Careful, Corey."

He looked up at her eagerly. "Want to go outside."

"We have to help Anna with dishes first."

Corey's face fell.

"Please," Brent cajoled Jessica.

Travis shoved his chair back. "I'll take them outside while you clean up if you'd like." He sounded as eager as the boys.

While Travis went upstairs to change from his suit, Ellie found the boys' snowsuits and she and Jessica dressed Corey and Brent for the outdoors. By the time the two were ready, they could barely walk for all the protective clothing.

Travis laughed. "They look like they're ready to walk on the moon."

Ellie couldn't help grinning. "Remember what it felt like to try to play in a snowsuit?"

"Do I. I had a red one, with a matching red hat that looked like an old cloth football helmet with a bill, and waterproof red mittens that were so slippery snowballs slid right off them."

"And the mittens were so stiff you couldn't pick up anything with them."

"And the muffler Mom tied around my face was so long it got caught beneath the sled runners."

It was fun sharing similar childhood memories, even though they hadn't known each other until college.

"Remember the snowball war we had our sophomore year in college?" Travis asked.

Ellie groaned. "You and me against your entire fraternity. How could I forget?"

"We didn't do so badly, considering."

"We came out of it alive, which is about the best one could say for that battle."

"Outside." Corey tried unsuccessfully to tug at Ellie's skirt with his mittened hands.

Ellie and Travis chuckled, their gazes meeting. An exciting thrill danced through her, like sparks on a sparkler, at the pleasure of sharing the moment.

Travis held out his gloved hands to the boys. "Come on, partners. Let's brave the elements."

"Okay, pa'dner," Corey agreed happily.

Ellie was sure the boys didn't understand Travis's words, but they knew he meant they were going outside together. Each lifted a hand trustingly and eagerly to Travis's, and the three went out the back door together.

When Ellie turned back to help Jessica and Anna with the dishes, she found Anna watching her with concern etched on her wrinkled face. "Are you sure you don't mind Travis living here, dear?"

"Of course not. I told you that when you asked me last week."

"I know, but with the trouble between the two of you. . ." The words trailed off. "You mean the world to me, Ellie. I won't have him here if it hurts you."

Ellie squeezed Anna's hands. "Thank you for caring, but it's fine. Travis needed a place to stay, and you had rooms to rent. He may not make a very good husband, but there's no reason he shouldn't make a good tenant." Travis's living arrangements were a bit uncomfortable for Ellie, but she wouldn't admit it to Anna. The older woman needed the money from the rent.

Ellie released Anna's hands and picked up a dish towel. "I hope Travis isn't making too much work for you."

"Not at all. I like him."

Ellie didn't respond. She wasn't sure she wanted her friends to like her estranged husband too much.

"I think he'll be a help to have around. He shoveled the walks and driveway for me after last night's storm." Anna plunged her hands into the dishwater.

Ellie wandered to the back door, looking out the window at

Travis and the boys while wiping the platter in her hand.

Jessica retrieved the platter. "It's dry. It's going to shine like a waxed car if you don't stop polishing it."

"They're building a snowman."

Jessica and Anna peered out, both grinning as the boys together attempted to roll a lopsided ball. The ball wasn't very large before its mass was too great for their combined muscles. Travis leaned over and helped them complete the snowman's stomach.

Reluctantly, Ellie and Jessica went back to help Anna.

Ellie kept returning to the door to check on the snowman's progress while helping with the dishes.

Finally Jessica threw up her hands in disgust. "This is the fifteenth time you've checked on them. You're wearing a rut in Anna's linoleum. Why don't you go outside and join them?"

"Yes, go ahead," Anna urged. "Jessica and I can finish up here."

Ellie refused. She forced herself to stand by the cupboard with Jessica and Anna.

They were almost done with the dishes when the back door opened. All three women turned around at the rush of cold air.

Corey stood panting in his blue and red snowsuit, his cheeks and nose bright red from the winter chill. "We need a cawwot, muvver."

Ellie stared at him. "A carrot?"

Corey frowned. Ellie sensed his impatience with her. "For his nose. We're makin' a snowman."

"Can we see it?" Jessica asked while Anna opened the refrigerator to procure a carrot.

"No. We're not done." He grabbed the carrot between his mittened hands and left, his snowsuit *sh-sh-sh-ing* as he walked.

Ellie turned to the other women. "I must design some decent boys' snowsuits for next winter's children's line, something practical that a child can move in easily."

"That should be easy," Jessica encouraged dryly. "That's

why no one's figured it out before this."

"Just because it's difficult doesn't mean it's impossible."

Only a couple minutes passed before the door opened again. This time all three males stood there. Ellie noticed Travis's cheeks and nose were as red as the boys', and his eyes as filled with fun.

"C'mon and see our snowman," Brent demanded.

"C'mon." Corey waved an arm, urging the women outside.

"C'mon." Travis imitated Corey's gesture.

Ellie, Jessica, and Anna hurried to put on their boots and coats while the boys waited impatiently. When they all finally went outside, the women admired the boys' handiwork loudly and profusely. The boys looked like they'd burst with pride, but no more so than Travis.

"His name's Snowy," Corey informed them.

"Where did you get the eyes?" Ellie asked.

"Over there." Corey pointed to the gravel driveway.

"They aren't really eyes. They're stones," Brent explained gravely.

"I like the hat." Jessica was struggling to keep her mouth straight.

"It's T'avis's," Corey told her.

Red berries from a nearby dogwood tree made up a crooked smile. Twigs worked for the skinny arms. Likely the world had seen more original snowmen, but none that were so dear in Ellie's eyes as this one created by her son, his father, and her son's friend. She blinked back sudden tears. "Good job, guys. Your snowman has everything but a belly button."

Corey's mouth formed a large "O." He turned to Travis. "What makes a bellybutton?"

Travis looked at a loss for a moment. "How about another stone?"

"Okay!" The boys stumbled through the snow, looking like penguins as they hurried toward the driveway, the only place in the snow-covered landscape where they could hope to find a stone. When they reached their goal, they plopped down on their knees to search.

Jessica and Anna decided to take a walk in the crisp air, leaving Ellie and Travis to watch the boys. Ellie was suddenly uncomfortable.

"The scenery here is beautiful," Travis said quietly. "The mountains look like they go on forever."

The village was built on a low mountain. The Blue Ridge Mountains of North Carolina and the Smoky Mountains of Georgia could be seen in the distance, row after row of snow- and pine-covered peaks. Ellie never grew tired of their beauty. "They seem to change every day," she told him. "Sometimes every hour as the sunlight and shadows change, or a storm moves in, or the fog settles or rises."

"It'll be fun to live in a place where it snows. In California, I had to go to the mountains to ski and snowboard. Now that I'm in the mountains, I can just go out the back door." He grinned at his own joke.

"Some people do ski or snowshoe to work when there's enough snow," she admitted, "but most people commute the way people in the rest of America do, by foot or car."

"Here's the belly button." Corey held up a round stone.

"Looks good," Travis approved. "Better put it on Snowy."

Corey shoved the stone into the round white belly. Brent gave the stone an extra push.

Ellie and Travis shared a chuckle.

Satisfied they'd completed the snowman to the best of their ability, the boys looked for other entertainment. Spotting the sled on which Ellie and Jessica had pulled the boys to church and then to Anna's that morning, Brent let out a whoop and headed toward it. Corey followed, stumbling and falling flat on his face in the snow, then pushing himself up and starting out again.

"Looks like he's a veteran at that," Travis commented.

"At what?"

"Falling and starting over."

"All kids are accustomed to that. It's when they're older

that the courage to try again is bred out of them."

"I guess you're right."

She felt his gaze on her, but kept her own on the boys. At Brent's urging, Corey had climbed on the wooden sled. He sat with his legs straight forward and his hands clutching the sled's sides, his face shining with eagerness for the ride ahead. Brent leaned into the rope with all his weight, the intensity of his effort showing in the way his face screwed into lines. The sled jerked forward half a foot, then another. The boys were as happy as if they were moving a hundred miles an hour.

I wish I had their courage, Ellie thought. It exhausted her to consider the effort she and Travis would need to put into working out a lifetime of sharing the parental responsibilities and joys of raising Corey.

"It was good to see you in church this morning, Ellie."

Travis's jump to the topic of church surprised her. It took her a moment to change her line of thought. "I've been going for years."

"Why? Did you think it was a good idea to raise Corey with a faith in God?"

"Of course, but I started attending for myself before Corey was born. I wasn't doing such a good job of figuring life out by myself. I knew I needed to find help. I found what I needed when I decided to trust God."

Travis's smile was broad. "Me, too. Amazing what a difference believing in Him makes, isn't it?"

Surprise shot her eyebrows up. "Are you saying that you believe in God?"

He nodded. "Yep. Best thing that ever happened to me."

His new faith was a wonderful thing, if it was real, Ellie thought. "What happened to your conviction that 'God can mind His business and I'll mind mine and we'll get along just fine?' "

"Same thing that happened to you, I guess. I found out I wasn't getting along fine without Him at all."

Ellie wished she could believe him. Was his declaration of

faith a way of convincing her, and maybe others, that he'd make a good father for Corey? Rather than take him at his word, she'd wait and watch. If his faith was real, his actions would show it over time.

The boys were getting nearer—Brent still bending into the rope for all he was worth, and Corey urging him on between giggles and lurches of the sled.

Travis shook his head at the scene. "I like to think I'm in pretty good shape, what with the skiing and jogging I do, but if I worked at anything as hard as Brent is working now, I'd wake up so stiff the next day I couldn't get out of bed."

"Brent's muscles won't even remember this tomorrow."

"I'm beginning to feel old."

Travis didn't look old to Ellie. He looked a lot better than she would have liked. He was altogether too attractive for a man she didn't trust.

"I wish I'd brought my camera." Ellie would have liked to have pictures not only of the boys, but more importantly of Corey with his father making this first snowman.

"Do you have pictures of Corey when he was younger?" Travis asked quietly.

Ellie laughed. "What kind of mother would I be if I didn't?"

Travis didn't smile. "May I see them sometime?"

Ellie's smile died. She'd been thoughtless not to realize he would want to see them. She should have offered to show them to him before this. "Of course."

"Tonight?"

She hesitated. She was already worn out emotionally from being so near him today. Maybe she needed a break before they spent more time together.

"Please, Ellie."

Why not? It wasn't as if he was inviting her out for an intimate evening. He'd be looking at pictures. How long could it take? "All right."

The boys finally reached them. Brent dropped the rope. He was panting so hard the pale blue snowsuit rose and fell over his chest. His face showed his complete satisfaction with his Olympian effort.

Travis patted him on the back. "Good job. You're mighty strong."

Brent beamed.

"More," Corey urged.

"How about if I pull both of you?" Travis picked up the rope. "Jump on, Brent."

Brent hastened to join Corey. The boys giggled in their anticipation.

Ellie watched Travis pulling the boys around the yard. Their calls urging Travis to "go faster, faster" were clear in the cold air. She was surprised they hadn't urged him to take them down one of the many steep hills in town. It probably wouldn't be long before they did. Or before Travis thought of it himself.

Could it be any more dangerous than the emotional mountains she and Corey were traveling by allowing Travis back in their lives? Shivering, Ellie wrapped her soft black muffler closer about her neck.

five

Corey and Brent were already in their pajamas when Travis arrived at seven that evening. "The boys are in the kitchen," Ellie explained. "Jessica is making hot chocolate."

"Hot chocolate?"

The hope in his eyes and voice showed clearly he'd like some hot chocolate, too. Ellie groaned inwardly. She didn't want to do anything to encourage him to stay longer than necessary. She was already regretting she'd agreed to meet with him. Oh, well, if he drank the hot chocolate while they looked at the albums, the drink shouldn't extend his visit. "I'll ask Jessica to make you a cup."

He grinned and pulled off his coat. "Thanks."

The swinging door between the kitchen and hall banged open. Corey barreled toward them in footed yellow fuzzy pajamas. "Hi, pa'dner." He threw his arms around one of Travis's legs.

"Hi, partner." Travis lifted Corey into his arms.

Ellie's heart lurched. The two were taking to each other altogether too quickly for her comfort. The thought sharpened her tone. "Jessica is waiting for you in the kitchen, Corey."

"Okay. Want hot choc'late, pa'dner?"

"Sure do."

"C'mon." Corey wiggled.

Travis got Corey's body language message and set him down.

"The albums are on the living room coffee table. You can drink your hot chocolate while you look at the pictures."

"No." Corey grabbed one of Travis's hands with both his own. "Dwink with me."

Ellie wasn't about to give in this time. "Travis can't stay

53

long." She felt Travis's gaze on her, and her face grew hot. She reached for Corey's hand. "You can say goodnight to Travis after you're done with your snack."

"No." Corey ignored her hand and tugged on Travis's. "C'mon."

Travis gently removed Corey's hold. "Mom's the boss."

Corey's lower lip trembled.

Travis squatted down. "I promise I won't leave until you've come in to say goodnight. Is it a deal?"

"Okay." Corey made it clear it wasn't a satisfactory deal.

Jess appeared in the dining room. "Hey, Corey, we almost forgot your favorite mugs. Are you going to help me get them down?"

"Yes." He hurried into the dining room. Travis followed.

Feeling defeated, Ellie trailed along.

Jess opened the china closet and lifted Corey so he could reach a porcelain mug shaped like an elephant. The elephant's trunk made the mug's handle.

He held it toward Travis. "Look."

"Wow. Great mug."

Jess pulled out another mug. "This one's Brent's." A giraffe's long neck made up the handle of Brent's mug.

Ellie closed the china closet doors. "Would you bring Travis and me some hot chocolate, too? No special mugs required."

Travis chuckled.

Corey decided someone must have said something funny. He threw back his head and laughed, watching for the adults' reaction. He wasn't disappointed.

When the laughs died down, Travis nodded at an old print hanging on the wall. It was of a log cabin on a snow- and pine-covered mountainside. "That looks like a romantic place."

Jess grimaced. "Not to me. My husband and I have a cabin that looks a lot like that. Former owners made moonshine in it."

Travis burst into laughter. "You're putting me on."

"Nope, but I promise your hot chocolate will be nothing but chocolate and milk." She carried Corey and the mugs into the kitchen.

At this rate it was going to be a long evening, Ellie thought. "Ready to look at the pictures?" She led the way back to the living room.

Travis swung a hand over the three albums on the coffee table. "Which is first?"

She handed him an album with a white satin cover trimmed in baby blue. "This one." She sat beside him on the worn blue sofa while he opened the book as though it contained a fragile treasure.

She heard his sharp intake of breath as he looked at the first page. The pictures were of Corey and herself in the hospital right after Corey was born. She felt suddenly vulnerable. She shrank away from him, sinking into the back of the sofa.

Travis ran one large, blunt, trembling index finger over a picture of a naked, wrinkled, screaming Corey, then over another of Corey wrapped in a blanket of palest blue and lying on her chest. "I should have been there for you, for both of you."

Her heart contracted at the words which had been spoken in a cracked whisper. Her gaze darted to his face. Was that tears causing his eyes to glisten?

He turned his head so their gazes met.

They are tears. It was as though they trickled into her heart.

Guilt flooded after them. He was right. He should have been there, holding newborn Corey. She'd deprived him of that experience and could never give it back.

Did Travis's arms ache for that loss? Was that the pain she saw in his eyes now? Her own arms ached to hold Travis and make the pain go away.

Ellie broke their eye contact, looking down at her lap.

I'm sorry. She pressed her lips hard together against the words. She was sorry, but if she said the words, he might misunderstand. He might think she was apologizing for leaving him, for no longer trusting him. She wasn't sorry for those things. It wasn't safe for her or Corey to trust him. She didn't want to give him any emotional ammunition to use against her. So she swallowed the words and tried to swallow her guilt, too.

From the corner of her eye she watched him turn the page. She gave her attention back to the album. Family pictures covered this page. Her family. Her mother holding Corey. Her father holding Corey. Her younger brother, Alan, holding Corey. Herself holding Corey and grinning from ear to ear. Only her family, her friends, not Travis's.

The guilt increased.

Jessica came in and set two steaming mugs on the coffee table, grinned at Ellie and Travis, and returned to the kitchen. Her entrance lessened Ellie's tension a trifle. She reached for the mug, glad to have something else to concentrate on.

Travis paged through the record of Corey's first few months of life: first day home, baby gifts, his first Easter, his first bath at home, his first bottle, his first time in a swing, his first time sitting up by himself, his first Christmas, in a stroller, in a playpen, crawling, his first steps—or maybe his second. Then there was Corey playing with his toes, playing with his toys, studying his belly button, laughing, crying, at the service dedicating him to God, and lots of pictures of Corey doing nothing but sleeping. Ellie gave brief explanations when necessary or in response to Travis's questions.

They'd just started on the second album when Corey hurried into the room.

He flung himself against Travis's knees. "You still here."

Travis ruffled Corey's golden curls. "Of course. Told you I would be."

If only his promises were that trustworthy, Ellie thought bitterly.

Corey struggled to climb up on the sofa. Travis lifted him effortlessly. The boy plopped down beside Travis, snuggling close to his father. Noting the pictures, Corey squealed in delight. "That's me!"

Travis frowned. "Are you sure? The boy in the pictures doesn't look old enough to be you."

"Uh-huh, is too." Corey's head bobbed up and down. "I was little."

"Really?"

"Uh-huh. I was one. See?" Corey shoved a pudgy finger over a picture of himself in a white short-sleeved top and white shorts seated beside a birthday cake with a single blue candle in the middle of it. "That's my bi'thday cake."

"Did you have a party?"

"Uh-huh."

"Who was at your party?"

Corey turned the page and pointed to people in the pictures as he rolled off, "Mommy an' Gwamma an' Gwampa an' Jessie an' Bwent."

Ellie watched the exchange silently, joy at the interaction between father and son braiding with regret and trepidation to form a confusing, bittersweet sensation.

"How old are you now?"

Corey held up two fingers.

Jessica and Brent came into the room holding hands. "Brent's going to bed now. We came in to say goodnight."

Ellie hugged Brent when he came over to her. "Goodnight. Sweet dreams. I love you."

"Love you." Brent looked at Travis, hesitating as if not certain how personal to be with him. Ellie knew he liked Travis, but he obviously wasn't as taken with the man as Corey was.

Travis gave him a grin. "I had fun building the snowman with you today. Maybe you'll let me play with you again sometime."

Brent nodded. A moment later he lifted his arms. Travis leaned forward and gave him a tight, quick, one-armed hug. "Good night."

" 'Night. Comin' Corey?"

Corey shook his head. "I'm showin' Twavis my pictures."

Ellie groaned inwardly. Usually Corey was good about

going to bed when he was asked to. She hated the battles when he didn't want to go, but she refused to let him win those battles. "It's your bedtime, Corey."

He shook his head harder and stared at the photo album, refusing to meet her gaze as though that refusal strengthened his position.

Jessica held out a hand. "Why don't you come upstairs with Brent and me? I'll read you a story after you're tucked in."

Corey repeated his silent battle.

Ellie sighed. Before she could say anything, Travis caught her gaze. The appeal in his for more time with his son was unmistakable. She caved in to guilt. "You can stay up for a few more minutes."

"Thanks." Travis smiled.

At first Corey eagerly told Travis about each succeeding picture, but it wasn't long before Corey was yawning. Travis slipped an arm around the boy, and he slumped against his father as he grew more tired.

Ellie could tell Travis was treasuring this time, the feel of his son resting against him in the manner all boys should be able to rest trustingly in their fathers' arms. But could Corey trust Travis? She'd discovered in a painful way that she could not. She didn't want that to happen to her son.

Soon Corey's explanations petered out. His head bobbed, then rested against Travis's chest.

Travis and Ellie exchanged amused glances as Corey struggled to stay awake, his eyes closing and opening repeatedly. Finally the battle was over. His eyes stayed closed, long lashes resting against round cheeks like pencil-thin shadows of trees against snow in moonlight.

"Should I carry him upstairs for you?" Travis whispered.

She started to say no, but then realized that putting his son to bed was another experience Travis hadn't had before, and she nodded.

They went up the stairs together. Ellie led the way to the bedroom the boys shared. A nightlight kept them from tripping over a few scattered toys as they crossed the room to Corey's crib.

Corey stirred slightly when Travis laid the boy down. Ellie took from the crib rail the teddy bear quilt her mother had made and placed it over Corey. She touched his cheek lightly, saying a silent prayer that the Lord would keep him safe throughout the night, the prayer she said every night.

At that moment she felt Travis's hand on her shoulder. Her heart jumped and began racing.

She couldn't move. The moment was too sweet, too much the ideal family scene as she'd pictured it when she was younger and naive, with parents gazing together adoringly at their sleeping child. A moment too precious not to savor in spite of the legacy of broken trust.

Travis's touch felt familiar even after three years. She'd always loved the gentleness in the way his large hands touched her. It had been hard after she left him to make herself refuse to remember his touch, refuse to remember what it felt like to be in his arms. Now memories flooded back, sending waves of longing through her.

He squeezed her shoulder and smiled tenderly at her.

She stepped back quickly before her body and emotions could betray her further and led the way from the room. Ellie tried to slow her breathing as she walked down the stairs, but it was difficult with Travis right behind her.

She walked directly to the tree rack, removed his jacket, and held it out to him. She forced herself to look him squarely in the eyes and smile, refusing to allow him to see how she was quaking inside from her desire to allow all the walls she'd built to fall down and let herself know the joy of his arms once more.

He didn't put the coat on. He crushed it between his hands, his gaze boring into hers. "Thank you."

Sincerity rumbled through the quiet words, weakening the foundation of the distance Ellie was trying to keep.

Travis cupped her cheek gently in one hand, sending

tremors through her. "Thank you for tonight, Ellie, for the pictures, for the time with Corey. Thank you for raising our son with such love." The last words were a whisper.

Travis's jacket dropped to the floor. One arm slid about Ellie's waist, pulling her slowly against him. The familiar scent of his Langenfeld cologne enveloped her.

Ellie knew she was going to be in trouble if she didn't stop him, but she couldn't make herself say no. The palms of her hands trembled against his chest. Some traitorous part of her wanted to feel his kiss again, to live in the dream of desire satisfied in loving and trusting this man.

Travis's hand on her cheek tenderly urged her face toward his. His lips touched hers, lightly, testing, warm. Then again, and she leaned into his kiss, welcoming it, remembering it.

It felt so good it was frightening.

She pulled her head back, breaking off the kiss, and closed her eyes. "No."

His forehead touched hers. His heart banged beneath her palms. "Okay." The word was barely more than a ragged breath.

Ellie lifted her hands from his chest and stepped back.

He released her instantly. Regret and relief washed through her as the warmth of his body was removed.

She tried to regain a semblance of control. "You can have the negatives if you want."

"Negatives?"

"Of the pictures of Corey."

"Oh, right, negatives."

"Do you want them?"

"I was just thinking."

"What?"

"I wouldn't need my own copies of Corey's pictures if we lived together as a family again."

Ellie stared at him in disbelief. The blood pounded in her ears so loud she was sure she'd misheard him.

"What do you say, Ellie? We're still married. All we'd have to do is move in together."

six

"You can't be serious." Ellie widened the gap between them.

Travis mentally kicked himself. He'd jumped in too fast. He should have known better. He did know better. Only everything had felt so good tonight, so right, with Ellie and Corey. His longing for them had outrun his judgment.

Now that he'd jumped in with both feet he might as well continue. He took a deep breath and plunged both hands through his hair.

"I am serious. I want to be with my son. And I've missed you like crazy."

"We can't just. . .just move in together again after all this time."

"How long do we have to wait to make it proper?"

"Maybe a lifetime. I'm not sure we should get back together."

Travis was terrified to ask the next question, which was the very reason he knew he must. "If that's the way you feel, why haven't you filed for divorce?"

"I. . .I don't know."

"I hoped it was because you still love me." How could admitting his need for his wife's love feel as terrifying as jumping out of a plane without a parachute?

Ellie rubbed her arms and refused to meet his gaze.

Travis swallowed hard. "Maybe it was because you were afraid if I found out about Corey I'd try to take him away from you."

Her head swung up.

The fright in her eyes made Travis sick to his stomach. "That's it, isn't it?"

"You can't take him away." The words were raspy with

fear. "I'm a good mother. There's no reason the courts would let you take him away from me."

He laid a hand on her upper arm in an attempt to calm her.

She jerked away.

"Sorry." Travis held up his hands, palms out. "I'd never take Corey away from you unless I thought it was necessary for Corey's well-being."

Ellie's eyes flashed.

Travis heart sank. Another bad error. He rushed on, hoping to divert her defensive anger. "I haven't any reason to believe you aren't a wonderful mother. That's what I'd expect you to be, a wonderful mother."

A little tension left her face, and he allowed himself a small sigh of relief. "We're both Christians now, Ellie. We're still married. I believe it's God's will families stay together. Don't you?"

"I can't trust you. How can I live with you when I can't trust you?"

"I tried to explain about Michelle before, but you wouldn't let me."

"I know what I saw, and I know what I heard. I trust my eyes and ears more than I trust your explanations. I'd be a fool not to."

"But—"

"I've no one to blame but myself for falling in love with a man who treated me the way you did, but I don't want Corey to be hurt by you, too."

Shock exploded inside Travis. "You can't think I'd hurt my own son."

"I want Corey to have a father he can trust, whose values don't include humiliating him in front of others, belittling his dreams and abilities, breaking promises, and betraying him." Ellie's eyes snapped with anger. Her hands formed into fists. "That's why I didn't tell you about Corey earlier. Every day since I mailed that letter I've worried that it was a horrible mistake. I can't keep you from seeing him, but I don't have to let you live with us and pretend we're a happy family. If I did, and you broke your trust again, the betrayal would be that much worse for Corey."

Travis felt like he'd been kicked in the stomach. "You think I can't be trusted? What about a mother who abandons the man she's promised to live with forever, who leaves without even saying good-bye? What about a mother who won't even try to work things out when there's a problem?"

"I did try, before you spent the night with that Michelle woman."

"Ellie, Travis, keep it down!"

Travis looked up in surprise to see Jessica leaning over the stairway banister in flannel pajamas. In a flash he realized he and Ellie had raised their voices to the point of yelling. He closed his eyes and rubbed his hands down over his face. "Did we wake the boys?"

"I didn't take time to find out. You woke me." Jessica's troubled gaze moved from Travis to Ellie. "You okay?"

Ellie nodded.

"Are you sure?" Jessica gave Travis a look that made him feel as if she was considering making a domestic violence report.

"I'm sure," Ellie said. "Sorry, Jess."

Travis dug his hands into the pockets of his khakis. "I'm sorry, too."

"Call me if you need me," Jessica ordered Ellie.

When Jess was back upstairs, Travis walked into the living room where their voices wouldn't carry upstairs as easily. Ellie followed. "I am sorry. I shouldn't have yelled," he admitted. "I think Jess is afraid I'll raise more than my voice."

"Her estranged husband has a mean temper. Dan beat her. That's why she left the marriage. She was afraid he'd start hitting Brent, too."

Travis gave a low whistle. "No wonder she's worried about me."

Ellie brushed her thick brown hair behind her ears. With a

catch in his chest he realized she looked suddenly tired. "Did you mean what you said? I never thought of it as abandoning you when I left. I was only protecting myself from being hurt by you further. I never saw it from your point of view."

"I guess both of us could have acted wiser." He felt miserable—about tonight, about what had happened between them three years ago, about the years they'd lost in between. Could they ever repair it all? "I still love you, Ellie. I've never stopped loving you."

"I want to believe you, but I don't dare let myself trust you. I'm so afraid you'll hurt me again, and more afraid you'll hurt Corey." Her eyes looked haunted. "Besides, I don't think love treats people the way we treated each other."

He hated the pain in her eyes. He wanted to hold her and make all the pain he'd caused her go away. The knowledge that his comfort was the last thing she'd accept right now intensified his own pain.

"Would you please leave?" She brushed her bangs back in a weary gesture. "I'm tired, and I don't want to argue any more."

He couldn't stay if she wanted him to leave. He picked up his coat from the floor. At the door he turned, studying her face. He wanted desperately to tell her again that he loved her. "Thanks again for tonight. It meant a lot to me."

He reflected on the evening while he walked the few blocks back to Anna's house, the crisp winter night quickening his steps as they squeaked on the snowy sidewalk. He'd made a huge blunder, suggesting he and Ellie get back together. He'd been moving way too fast.

He groaned, remembering the way it felt to hold her again, the feel of her hair soft against his cheek, the gentle floral scent she wore, her lips soft beneath his, hesitating before they yielded to his invitation, then drawing back. It was going to be harder slowing down again now that he'd held her.

How was he ever going to get past the pain he'd inflicted on her? "Lord, show me how to convince her she can trust my love."

What had she said right before he left? "I don't think love treats people the way we treated each other."

I'll just have to prove my love for her a day at a time, a step at a time. Baby steps.

❧

Ellie found it difficult concentrating on work at the boutique the next morning. The memory of the kiss she and Travis had shared kept getting in the way. If only it hadn't felt so good. Ellie groaned.

Jessica looked up from the sketch she was showing Ellie for a necklace of dogwood blossoms in silver. "What's the matter?"

"Nothing. This sketch looks great. Could you make a bracelet to match?"

"Sure. It's Travis, isn't it?"

"What's Travis?"

Jessica's bracelets jangled as she propped her fists on her narrow, jean-covered hips. "The groan. Your absentminded attitude this morning. You're thinking about the argument you had with Travis."

"Not really." Ellie's lips lifted in a slow smile.

Jessica's eyes narrowed. "I don't think I like that twinkle in your eyes. What exactly happened last night? The part I didn't hear when you were yelling at each other, that is."

"I think Travis proposed to me."

"He can't propose to you. You're already married."

"It sounded a lot like a proposal. He wants us to live together again."

"That's indecent."

"It isn't indecent. Like you said, we're already married."

"Ellie, get a grip. This is the man who cheated on you. You aren't going to let him hurt you that way again, are you?"

"No." Ellie examined the wonderful blue and green fabric on her worktable. "I dreamed that he and I were back together. When I woke up I could almost feel his arms around me. My first thought was how in the beginning of our marriage we would fall asleep with his arm around my shoulders and my cheek against his chest. Sometimes I miss that, you know?"

"I do know." A wistfulness slipped into Jessica's tone, like fog softening the edges of jagged mountain bluffs. "Sometimes I wonder if I'll ever experience that with anyone again." She picked up Ellie's open shears, clapped them shut, and slammed them down on the work table. "But I never make the mistake of thinking I can have true intimacy with Dan, or with any other man who beats women. And you can't have it with a man you can't trust, either."

"I guess. . .it feels nice to be wanted again."

"Ellie—"

"Don't worry. I told Travis we can't live together, that I don't trust him not to hurt me and Corey."

"Good. We all hurt others without trying to. It's when people do it on purpose it's a problem. When a man cheats on his wife, he's hurting her on purpose."

"I know." Ellie wished Jess would stop repeating that Travis had cheated on her. She hated those words and the emotions they evoked.

A question she'd pushed away repeatedly popped into her mind. Why hadn't Travis filed for divorce so he could marry Michelle? Maybe he didn't think he needed to, since he'd been seeing her while he was married to Ellie anyway.

"You have to protect yourself and Corey. Especially Corey. You're the adult. If you want to let yourself in for a life filled with pain, no one can stop you." Jessica threw her arms up in a gesture of disgust, her bracelets saucily adding their tinkling music. "Corey hasn't a choice in the matter. You're the only one who can limit the pain he's exposed to."

Ellie sighed and dropped her head into her hands. "I know you're right."

"If all you're looking for is a man to make you feel wanted, what about Chuck? Lately I've had the impression all he's waiting for is for you to give him an indication you're a teeny bit interested in him."

"Chuck is nice, but I'm married to Travis."

"Maybe you shouldn't be."

"Maybe." Ellie had gone back and forth on this issue for three years. She had friends who knew a lot more about the Bible than she did who believed God never allowed divorce, and others who believed He allowed it in certain circumstances. She respected what others believed for themselves. She certainly felt Jessica had been wise to leave Dan to protect herself and Brent. For herself Ellie only knew she'd promised to love and stay married to Travis for the rest of their lives. Even knowing he'd been unfaithful, she wasn't quite ready to sever her ties with him completely. She knew people who would consider her emotionally unhealthy because of that, but that's where she stood.

The tinkle of brass bells and the laughter of young women announced new customers. Ellie glanced into the shop. She didn't recognize the women. They were probably visitors at the nearby ski resort, as so many of her customers were this time of year.

"I'll wait on them," Jessica offered. "I know you want to get this outfit cut out." She entered the shop with her usual quick pace and greeted the women warmly.

Ellie turned gratefully to her work. She'd asked Anna to watch Corey and Brent today so she and Jessica could work on some one-of-a-kind spring pieces. She hadn't put many spring pieces out in her shop yet, but she was well aware major department stores had already cleared out much of their winter merchandise and were filling the space with spring outfits. Most of her designs were ready to be hung out.

This gorgeous silk material was for a summer, ankle-length shift and shawl. The color was a rich blending of blue and green, with a jewel-like depth to it. The material was so soft it felt like she remembered the water of a lake feeling against her skin on a calm summer day.

Ellie had a moment of regret. It would be fun to make the gown for herself. She'd designed the dress for Jewell Landry, a wealthy local woman, one of Ellie's most loyal customers and one of her best advertisements. Every time Mrs. Landry wore one of Ellie's outfits, women came into the shop asking for similar outfits. Since Mrs. Landry insisted everything she purchased be one of a kind, Ellie never had exactly the same thing available, yet she seldom sent these women away empty handed after they'd seen her stock.

Humming to herself, Ellie pinned her hand-cut tissue paper pattern to the material. She was glad Anna had agreed to watch the boys at home today. There were too many dangerous things in the workroom, she thought, picking up her expensive shears.

Jessica bounced into the workroom, brushing the palms of her hands back and forth, obviously pleased with herself. "They bought one of those wonderful cardigans with the mountain design, and a blue tweed suit, and a pale blue silk blouse with one of Anna's lace collars."

"That is a good sale." Those were among Ellie's most expensive winter pieces.

"Here we go again," Jessica said as the brass bells gave the message of a new arrival. "Here's hoping they're in as much of a buying mood as the last customers."

She swung about and stopped. "It's Dan."

"Oh, no, Jess."

"Some customers came in right behind him."

"I'll wait on them. Why don't you ask Dan to come back here to talk? Just be careful."

"He won't hurt me in a public place." Jessica went to meet him.

Ellie wasn't so sure. She started toward the door to the shop, turned around, and stuck her scissors into her skirt's deep pocket, then hurried to greet her customers.

"Hi, Dan." She gave him what she hoped appeared a welcoming smile when they passed each other. He'd think up enough reasons to act obnoxious without her encouraging him by being unfriendly.

The customers were a middle-aged woman and her teenage daughter, again taking a break from the ski slopes. They chatted pleasantly with Ellie in between exclaiming over her sweater collection.

Ellie's stomach tightened in dread anticipation when she first heard the angry rumble of Dan's deep voice, too loud for normal conversation. She sent up a silent prayer for God to protect Jessica and give her wisdom in her words so that she would not anger Dan unnecessarily. Not that the man needed a reason to act angrily.

The customers darted curious glances toward the workroom, and Ellie's stomach cinched tighter.

Dan's voice suddenly became almost inaudible. The women's attention went back to the soft sweaters before them. Ellie stole a glance toward the back of the shop. The swinging door separating the shop and workroom had been closed. Ellie didn't know whether she felt relieved or not. She was glad Dan was no longer disturbing her customers, but the closed door made Jessica more vulnerable to Dan's anger.

The daughter decided on a pale peach sweater with a heart-shaped pocket and matching silver heart-shaped buttons designed by Jessica. The sweater had been one of Ellie's most popular with teenage girls that season. Ellie was ringing up the sale when Mrs. Landry entered the shop.

When Ellie handed her customer her package, she looked relieved to hurry out of the shop with her daughter.

Ellie put on her most professional smile. "Hello, Mrs. Landry."

"I just stopped by to see how my new gown is coming."

"I started cutting it out this morning. It's in the workroom."

Dan's voice rose again. Ellie's heart plummeted. Mrs. Landry was the last person Ellie wanted to have hear his tirade in her store.

Her customer frowned. "What is going on back there?"

Ellie spread her hands, searching her mind for an answer that wouldn't reveal things Jessica preferred remain private.

Chuck walked in just in time to give her a reason not to answer.

Dan's voice had risen so loud that Mrs. Landry looked uneasy. There'd been a couple thuds and thunks Ellie hadn't liked the sound of, either.

Ellie hurried across the room to Chuck. His smiling greeting quickly turned to a frown as he became aware of Dan's bellowing.

"Dan?" he asked before Ellie had a chance to say anything.

"Yes."

He started toward the back room. She stopped him with a hand on his arm. "Please," she urged in a low voice, "will you get the sheriff?"

He looked toward the back room uncertainly.

"Please, Chuck. Hurry."

He pressed his lips together and left, angry determination in every stride.

Ellie breathed a sigh of relief. The sheriff's office was on the next block. Help should arrive any minute.

She started toward the back room. Mrs. Landry clutched Ellie's arm with a well-manicured hand. "Be careful."

Ellie opened the swinging door slowly, not knowing whether Jessica or Dan was behind it. Entering the room, her gaze immediately searched out Jessica. She was on the opposite side of the room, the large worktable between her and Dan. Ellie felt as though she could collapse in relief when she saw her friend apparently hadn't been hit.

Dan's face was red with unrepressed fury. He glared at Ellie and barked, "This is a private discussion."

"Not that you'd notice." Ellie pushed the door back and locked it open. She hated to expose Jessica to Mrs. Landry's curiosity, but she didn't dare leave her friend alone with Dan any longer.

Mrs. Landry stayed back by the counter, stretching her neck to see. Dan didn't notice her.

Ellie leaned back against the door. One sweeping glance

told her what had caused the noises she'd heard earlier. Her dress form was on the floor, as was the beautiful material with which she'd been working and numerous supplies.

Dan grabbed the edge of the door. "Get out of here." His voice was jagged-edged with anger.

The brass bells jangled.

"More customers," Ellie announced, not leaving her post. Maybe he'd be too embarrassed to continue acting out his anger if he knew people could see who was making all the noise.

Dan glanced into the shop. His mouth tightened. He jammed his hands into the pockets of his brown suit coat.

Ellie followed his glance. Travis was coming toward her, a bounce in his step and a smile on his face. "Hi, Ellie. I was hoping we could have lunch together."

He gave Dan a short curious look, started to greet Jessica, and stopped short, taking in the mess in one sweeping glance. "What happened in here?"

No one answered.

Travis looked at Ellie with raised eyebrows.

She bit her bottom lip. If she said anything, it might set Dan off again.

His eyes narrowed as he looked at Dan. "I don't think we've met. I'm Travis Carter, Ellie's husband." He didn't offer his hand.

"Dan Robbins, Jessica's husband." Dan's chin jutted out belligerently.

"Soon to be ex," Jessica reminded him.

Travis eyes widened a sliver and Ellie knew the information was registering, that he was remembering what she'd said about Dan being an abusive husband. "Are you okay, Jess?"

Jessica nodded and knelt down to gather up the blue and green silk.

"Jess and I were having a private conversation. If you two will leave, we'll finish it." Dan jerked at the door behind Ellie, causing Ellie to stumble forward.

Travis caught her. She felt the strength in his arm as he drew her against him.

"Don't do that again." Travis's words were a quiet threat.

The two men glared at each other. Dan was the first to look away. "If you'll just leave us alone a couple more minutes. . ."

"I don't think we'll be doing that." Travis's voice was still quiet and even. "Ellie and Jess obviously have work to do in here."

The front door crashed open. Chuck rushed in, a sheriff in an official brown jacket right behind him with one hand on his holster.

Thank You, Lord. Ellie's stomach muscles slackened the tautness that had started when Dan entered the shop.

Chuck stopped just outside the back-room door. Mrs. Landry moved quickly to stand behind him, peeking over his shoulder into the room.

Ellie watched Sheriff Eric Strand take in Jessica's condition and the condition of the room in a moment.

"Jess, Dan, Ellie, Travis." Sheriff Strand greeted them with cautious friendliness.

Ellie was surprised he knew Travis, then realized of course a law officer would be familiar with even the newest of the town's lawyers.

"Any trouble here?" The sheriff's eyes questioned each of them in turn.

Dan's chin jutted out again. "No trouble." He caught sight of Mrs. Landry and Chuck, and Ellie saw him struggle to gain some composure.

"Jess?" The sheriff singled her out.

Jess shook her head. She still had the work table between herself and her estranged husband. Her arms were crossed tightly over her chest, as though she were hugging herself to feel safe. Ellie's heart went out to her.

Sheriff Strand looked pointedly at the items Dan had knocked onto the floor. "Things are kind of a mess here, Ellie. Anything damaged?"

"I don't think so." The material for Mrs. Landry's dress probably needed cleaning, but it didn't seem worth mentioning. The sheriff was probably talking about the kind of damage for which Dan could be charged, and Ellie doubted the material qualified.

Chasing off Ellie's customers with his angry, loud voice likely wasn't a chargeable offense, either. Jessica's soon to be ex-husband probably couldn't be charged for anything he'd done today, unless it was disturbing the peace.

"It's almost noon, Dan. How about if we have lunch together? It's on me." Sheriff Strand laid a hand on Dan's arm.

Dan shook it off under the guise of straightening his suit coat. "Thanks, I have other plans for lunch." He stalked out of the room and out of the shop without looking back.

Ellie drew a shaky breath. "Thanks, Eric."

"Any time." The sheriff looked from Ellie to Jess. "Either of you decide there's something you think Dan should be charged with, let me know." He lowered his chin, raised thick eyebrows, and stared pointedly at Jess. "I mean it. Don't you let him get away with anything he shouldn't. Man with a temper like Dan's is dangerous."

"I know." Misery looked out of Jess's eyes.

Ellie's heart wanted to burst at the sight of it.

The sheriff left, looking dissatisfied with the results of his call. He offered his arm to Mrs. Landry. "Why don't we let the ladies get things organized again, Mrs. Landry? Then they'll be able to devote all their time to you."

Ellie was glad to see her wealthy customer leave with Sheriff Strand, though Mrs. Landry looked back over her shoulder until they reached the outside door.

Throughout the sheriff's questioning Chuck had stood just outside the workroom door. Now he asked quietly, "You sure you're okay, Ellie?"

"I'm fine." It was only then she realized she was still standing in the safe circle of Travis's arm. Blood raced to her face. She stepped away from Travis. She could feel his gaze on her as his arm fell away, but she refused to meet it.

Curiosity and something which looked suspiciously like pain filled Chuck's eyes as they studied hers. Angry with herself for feeling compromised for being in her husband's arms in what had been a dangerous situation, she put more warmth than necessary into her appreciation. "Thanks for getting Eric for us, Chuck."

She moved quickly around the table to where Jessica was picking things up from the floor. Ellie's heart contracted at the way her friend was trembling. "It's okay. I'll pick it up later."

Jess shook her head hard. "It's my fault. I'll clean it up."

"It isn't your fault."

"If it weren't for me, Dan wouldn't have been here."

"He's responsible for his actions, not you. You know that. Why don't you go get some lunch, or go home and lie down for awhile?" Ellie slipped an arm around Jess's shoulder and gave her a loving squeeze.

"I'm sorry he got so loud." Tears filled Jessica's green eyes. "Did the customers say anything?"

"No." Not for the world would Ellie admit the customers' horrified looks or that Dan's angry voice had frightened customers away. "What was he so upset about this time?"

"Same old, same old." Jess's voice cracked, betraying her in her attempt at lightness.

"He wants to get back together with you," Ellie clarified.

"He's using Brent as a threat if I don't agree."

"What do you mean by 'threat'?" Travis asked sharply.

Jessica's slim shoulders lifted her white cotton sweater in a shrug. "The usual, I guess. He says if I don't agree to get back together with him, he will sue for full custody of Brent."

"What makes him think he could win?" The lawyer in Travis was in full force now.

"He's a professional with a good income. He can afford to give Brent anything he needs. I, on the other hand, couldn't make ends meet on my income from my jewelry and working here if Ellie and I didn't live together and share expenses."

"You give Brent a good and love-filled home," Travis assured her. "No judge would give Dan full custody based on what you just told me." His brows drew together. "From what Ellie told me, I thought. . .didn't you ever have Dan charged for hitting you?"

Her face flushed. "No."

"It sounded like Sheriff Strand knew about. . .the situation."

"It's no secret Dan has a bad temper and a loud, vile mouth. Some people suspect him of hitting me, but I've only admitted it to Ellie, Anna, and Chuck. I needed someone to know in case. . .in case something happened to me and I couldn't be there to protect Brent."

"Why didn't you report Dan?" Travis persisted.

Jessica straightened some of the supplies she'd picked up from the floor. "He said if I reported him he'd hurt Brent."

"You could have had a restraining order issued against Dan."

"Do you honestly think that would keep Brent safe from Dan?" Jessica's eyes flashed with disdain.

Travis looked like he wanted to argue for the system, but couldn't. "No."

"People who haven't been in relationships with people like Dan don't understand," Jessica asserted. "They think the solution is so easy. Just walk away. Just report him. Well, it isn't so easy to walk away knowing there isn't any way the law can protect you and your children from a man who wants to harm you."

A customer entered the shop and Ellie reluctantly left her friend with Travis, closing the door to the workshop. Chuck was still in the shop, too, she discovered. He appeared to be examining his workmanship on the display shelves he'd put in a couple of months ago.

The customer wanted to browse, so Ellie made herself busy straightening displays where she would be readily available if the customer had questions. No questions were asked. The customer soon left without making a purchase.

The door hadn't closed behind her before Chuck was at Ellie's side at the sales counter. "What exactly happened here?"

Ellie gave him a brief explanation. "I was afraid Dan would hurt Jess. She says he'd never do that in public. She's probably right. He'd know his reputation would be finished in this town if he was convicted of beating his wife."

Chuck snorted. Ellie suspected he was biting back a few choice words about Dan. Jessica had discussed the situation with Ellie and Chuck many times. Neither of them had been able to change Jessica's mind about the manner in which she dealt with Dan. They just tried to never leave their friend or Brent alone with Dan and listened when Jessica needed to talk to someone.

Chuck stuffed his hands into his pockets. "About when I came in," he started. "The second time, I mean."

"Yes?" Ellie encouraged when he stopped.

"I thought you and your husband weren't back together."

"We're not." A hint of reserve stiffened her spine.

"It kind of looked like you are."

"He only had his arm around me because—" She caught herself. She didn't owe Chuck or anyone else an explanation. "We're not back together." She stared back at him boldly. What did she have to hide?

"I stopped to ask if you wanted to go to lunch."

"I don't think I can today, not after what happened. Jess will probably need to get away for a while. Anna is watching the boys, so I can't ask her to come down."

"Another time."

"Sure."

There was an awkward silence.

Ellie tried to get past it. She didn't want anything to destroy their friendship. "Thanks again for coming to the rescue with Sheriff Strand."

He nodded. "I'll see if there's anything I can do to help in the back."

"Thanks." Ellie genuinely liked and respected him, but it was growing more evident all the time that he no longer wanted to keep their relationship on a platonic level. She certainly wasn't ready to move on to anything else. She doubted her beliefs would ever allow her to, regardless of what happened between her and Travis.

The relief she'd felt when Travis came into the shop, the security she'd known with his arm around her, washed over her. She'd known she and Jessica could rely on him.

Rely on him. The thought stopped her hands on the sales slips she was riffling through. Relying on him sounded awfully similar to trusting him. Of course, this situation was nothing like Travis choosing to be with another woman. Faithfulness in one way didn't ensure faithfulness in another.

Still, she discovered she was profoundly grateful she never had to fear Travis would physically harm her or Corey. No question that adultery was a betrayal, but what could possibly be worse than worrying that your child might be harmed by his father?

Travis came out of the workroom and stopped beside her. His face still looked tense. "Are you all right?"

"Yes."

"I hadn't realized Jess's husband was the Dan I knew through work. Even though our law firm had wealthy clients who were abusers, I always picture violent men as biker types, not professionals."

"It would be nice if we could tell by looking at someone whether they'd hit us or rob us." *Or have extra-marital affairs,* she thought. She changed the topic. "I'm glad you came by when you did, though."

"I am, too. I expect it wasn't a coincidence. Our heavenly Father probably had something to do with the timing."

Ellie grinned. "I expect He did."

"And here I thought I was only coming by to ask you out to lunch."

"I can't leave the shop."

"Is Corey with Anna today?"

"Yes, and Brent, too." Ellie laughed. "Anna has a lot of energy for a woman her age, but she'll probably be 'tuckered,' as she says, by the time Jess and I pick up the boys."

Travis's blue eyes grew darker and his jaw tensed. She wondered what she'd said to disturb him, then decided she'd imagined the reactions, for his next words gave no hint of anger.

"Maybe I'll stop home for lunch and give Anna a break. I like having lunch with our son, anyway."

A pleasant tingle ran through Ellie as it always did when he referred to Corey as "our" son. "One of Anna's homemade meals doesn't have anything to do with your plans, I'm sure," she teased.

"Her cooking is quite an incentive," he admitted lightly, "but not quite on par with Corey's company. See you later."

Ellie's fingers rested lightly against the wooden counter while she watched him leave, watched as he passed the shop's windows on his way to Anna's, noting the swing of his strong shoulders, remembering the safety she'd felt with his arm taut around her in the workroom.

And the familiarity she'd known in his arms last night. The memory of the kiss they'd shared warmed her with its sweetness. It had awakened the longing for the intimacies they'd shared in the early, happy days of their marriage.

She sighed deeply. She shouldn't have allowed the kiss. Any physical intimacy between them would only complicate matters.

But it had felt so good.

"Hi."

Jessica's arrival at Ellie's side jolted her from her reverie. "Hi, yourself. You doing okay?"

"Yeah. A little shaky still, but that will pass. I, uh, was talking to Travis. . ."

"Yes?"

"Maybe I misjudged him. A little. Maybe."

Ellie frowned. "What do you mean?"

"Maybe every guy who raises his voice in an argument isn't going to raise his fists, too."

"I really don't think Travis would ever strike me or Corey," Ellie said gently.

"Maybe not. It's hard to trust any man not to act violently, though. When Dan and I first started dating, he treated me like a princess. I never expected I'd one day be a. . .a battered wife." She wrinkled her nose. "It's still hard to use that term about myself."

"It's in the past. You were a battered wife. Now you're a wiser, stronger woman."

"Thanks." Jessica gave Ellie a quick hug. "Travis offered to represent me for free. He wants me to tell him everything I can remember that Dan's done, in the way of hurting me and such."

"Sounds like a good idea."

"Yeah. He seems like an okay guy. Except. . .except I guess you still can't trust him not to. . .you know."

Her words trickled through Ellie's veins like poison, killing her heart's tender new shoots of hope. "Yes. I know."

seven

As soon as Travis was out of sight of the shop, he set off in a jog. His heart was already beating as hard as though he'd run ten miles. He had to get to Corey and Brent. Dan's anger likely escalated when his ego was bruised, knowing so many people saw him out of control. What if he decided to take it out on Brent? Only fragile Anna would stand between the three-year-old and the furious man.

The slick soles on Travis's wing-tips slipped on a patch of ice, sending him crashing to the sidewalk. He picked himself up and took off again. He wished he'd worn his sneakers or sure-soled boots to work today.

He wished he'd taken the car to work instead of walking the few blocks between his office and Anna's.

He wished he hadn't worn his long camel hair coat over his suit today; it caught the wind and slowed his speed.

He wished fear wasn't tying his stomach into knots and building that hard ball at the base of his throat that made it hard to breathe as he ran.

He wished his law experience hadn't left him with too many vivid memories of what out-of-control dads could do to their own kids.

Prayers he couldn't express in words wafted heavenward while his feet flew over the snow-edged sidewalks.

He raced up the wooden steps, across the porch, flung open the front door, and rushed into the house. The design of the home was almost identical to Ellie's, and he could see from the front hall through the living room into the dining room—where three pairs of eyes stared at him in surprise.

Travis halted, his hand still on the open door's brass knob. His lungs all but collapsed from relief. Brent was fine. Corey and Anna were fine. Obviously Dan hadn't been here. *Thank You, Lord.*

He wanted to pull both boys into his harms, hug them hard, and never let them go, never allow them into a place where they could be harmed.

"Travis?" Anna's voice was a mixture of concern and amusement.

He was suddenly aware of how strange his bursting into the house that way must appear. He raised a hand, feeling sheepish. "Hi. Okay if I join you for lunch?"

Anna pushed back her chair. "Of course. We're having tomato soup and grilled cheese sandwiches. It will take only a couple minutes to heat some for you."

"Thanks." Travis closed the door, looking for the lock as he did so. There was only a key hole in the original, ornate brass door handle plate—a key hole Travis suspected hadn't seen a key since the house was built.

He started for the kitchen, surprised to find himself panting. He made time to jog each day. Normally the run from the boutique to Anna's house would cause his breath or heart rate to rise only slightly. Amazing the effect fear had on the body.

Anna was already at the stove. He moved quickly across her cheerful blue and white kitchen to check out the back door. Only a simple hook lock. He fastened it.

Anna stared at him with a puzzled expression, a spatula in one hand. Her gaze slipped to his feet, where a small muddy puddle was forming, then back to his face. "You're acting strangely."

He grimaced. "Sorry, forgot to take off my shoes." He slid them off.

"Is something the matter?"

He could have kicked himself for being so transparent. He hadn't meant to frighten her, but maybe it was safer if she were a bit frightened. He glanced into the dining room. The boys were laughing and chatting.

Travis moved close to her so that the boys wouldn't overhear and told her about Dan's outburst and Travis's worry for the boys.

"I've been concerned for Jessica ever since she told me about Dan's abuse." Anna's eyes were troubled beneath a furrowed brow. "But it never occurred to me Dan might show up here."

"Does he know you watch Brent sometimes?"

She shrugged. "I suppose so."

"Do you have keys for your doors?"

"No. I've never seen the keys, though my late husband's parents built this house."

"Would you mind having locks put on?"

"No, not under the circumstances."

Travis didn't want to leave her alone with the boys even for the time it would take to run to the local hardware store and pick up some locks. "If it's all right with you, I'd like to call Chuck and ask him to bring some locks up. Maybe he can put them on right away."

She swung a hand toward the wall beside the dining room door. "There's the phone."

Hand on the phone, he turned to her. "You're handling this pretty well. I thought you'd be more upset."

"You mean because I'm an old lady?"

He grinned in surprise at her description of herself. He'd never have had the nerve or lack of tact to call her that to her face. "A sweet little lady," he qualified.

"Sweet little old ladies don't grow to be sweet little old ladies without living through a lot of troubled times. That's why there's nothing tougher than a sweet little old lady." She winked at him.

He laughed and lifted the receiver. He reached Chuck on his cell phone and the carpenter readily agreed to come.

Next Travis called his temporary secretary and let her know he would be late getting back to the office. *Good thing I don't have any appointments this afternoon,* he thought, entering the dining room.

The boys greeted him with an enthusiasm that made his

heart expand with gratitude for the gift of having them in his life. He'd met his son a little over a month ago and been in town only a few days, and already he could barely remember what his life had been like before Corey.

He reached over and rubbed Corey's blond curls. "Hi, partner." Then he did the same with Brent's straight, thick brown hair.

Both boys giggled.

Travis loved the funny little-boy sound and the tiny-toothed grins that went along with it. Joy spiraled through him. "So what have you two been doing all day?"

"We went shoppin' with Anna," Brent announced.

Corey nodded, speaking around his grilled cheese sandwich. "For groc'ies."

"I'll bet she was glad you two helped her out with that chore."

Both boys nodded. "She didn't let us take the sled, though," Brent said.

"Too bad." Travis imagined it would be hard for Anna to pull both boys and carry the groceries at the same time, and the boys could hardly pull each other the few blocks to the store and back.

"We made cookies." Corey's wide-eyed grin showed he thought Travis should be especially impressed with this feat.

"Can I have one?"

Corey nodded.

"Have to clean your plate first," Brent qualified.

Travis swallowed a laugh. "It's a deal." He dipped his spoon into his soup.

"Here." Corey grabbed a handful of oyster crackers from the blue-and-cream pottery bowl in the middle of the table and dropped them into Travis's soup.

"Thanks." Travis rubbed a hand across his mouth, hiding another laugh. The boys each had so many of the small crackers in their bowls that he could barely see the soup.

"Look. You can do this." Corey pushed a cracker down into

his soup with the bottom of his spoon.

Brent did the same thing.

In a moment it turned into a contest as to which boy could push the most crackers down the fastest.

Travis's heart seemed to reach outside himself and hug both the boys. They were like brothers. Living together, they must feel like brothers. If anything happened to Brent, it would break Corey's heart.

And his own, Travis realized. Amazing how quickly a boy could take root in a man's heart.

Bang!

Travis leaped to his feet as the front door crashed open. His heart lodged in his throat. Had Dan found them?

He was dimly aware of Anna's gasp.

The boys' heads swivelled toward the door.

It wasn't Dan standing at the door.

"Ellie!" Travis dashed to her. Grabbed her arms. Looked her over, searching for any sign of harm. "Are you all right?"

She nodded, barely paying him any attention. Her gaze looked over his shoulder.

Travis knew she was reassuring herself the boys were safe. "They're fine," he told her in a quiet voice that wouldn't carry to the boys.

She braced herself against his chest then, gulping huge breaths of air. Corey was calling to her eagerly, but she spoke first to Travis. "I was so worried. It suddenly occurred to me that Dan might have come here when he left the shop. I got here as fast as I could."

Her unbuttoned coat and windblown hair were evidence of that fact. "I had the same idea. Better say hi to Corey."

Ellie hugged the boys and listened with rapt attention as they repeated their tale of their morning adventures. After a couple of minutes they were willing to share her with Travis and Anna again.

"Won't you join us for lunch?" Anna asked when the three adults entered the kitchen where they could talk privately.

"There's plenty of soup, and it won't take a minute to make another sandwich."

"Thank you, but I must get back to the shop."

Travis was instantly alert. "Is Jess there alone?"

She shook her head. "One of the women who knits my sweaters came by. I asked her to help Jessica out until I get back. I didn't say where I was going. I was afraid she'd insist on heading here herself, and if Dan was here, that might have only made things worse."

"You're probably right," Travis agreed.

"As long as I know you are all right, Ellie," Anna said, "I'll return to the dining room. I don't like to leave the boys alone too long."

Travis told Ellie he'd contacted Chuck to put locks on Anna's doors. "Do you and Jess have good locks on the doors at your house?"

"Yes, that was the first thing we did when we moved in. A lot of people in Blackberry don't lock their homes, but we didn't want Dan to stroll in unannounced."

"I don't remember the doors being locked when I've been there."

"I guess we don't always remember. We've become a bit too secure after all these months."

"It's time you start remembering."

Ellie eyes widened at the sharpness in his tone.

He winced. "Sorry, it's just that I don't want anything to happen to any of you."

"You're right, we should be more careful. When a person's as volatile as Dan, you never know when something might set him off. From now on we'll lock the doors as soon as we enter the house as well as whenever we leave."

"Good girl."

"That sounds like I'm a dog."

Travis laughed. "You are definitely not a dog." He wished he dared tell her how beautiful she was to him. "Be careful."

She wrinkled her brow and tilted her head to one side.

"How long are you planning to stay here? Don't you have to be at your office?"

"I told my secretary I won't be back for awhile. I won't leave until Chuck arrives."

"Thank you." Ellie's voice was so thick with gratitude that it felt like a hug.

After Ellie left, Travis found the old-fashioned dining room in the midst of transformation. Anna and the boys were spreading quilts over the dining-room table. The colorful bedding hung to the floor and was weighted down on the tabletop with large books. "What's going on?"

"Makin' a fo't," Corey informed him.

"A fort?"

"Uh-huh." Corey dropped to his hands and knees, lifted a quilt, and crawled beneath the table. A moment later he stuck his head out, the quilt draping it like a heavy peasant shawl. "See?"

Brent immediately followed suit.

Travis and Anna left the boys to their play and went into the living room. Anna sat down in a tapestry covered rocking chair from the turn of the century and picked up some handwork.

"What's that?" Travis asked, more to make conversation than from true curiosity.

"A raffia purse. Ellie asked me to crochet some for the shop. She thinks they'll be popular with the customers this summer."

Hands in his pockets, he watched her nimble fingers. "Ellie's doing pretty well with that store, isn't she?"

"Wonderfully. She has a true gift. She knows how to take the picture of an outfit or accessory in her mind and turn it into the real thing. Not everyone can do that. She's a shrewd businesswoman, too."

Travis didn't like the shame that crawled through him when he remembered the way he'd belittled Ellie's talents in the past.

He examined an old oil painting hanging above a camel-back sofa.

"My ancestors, Samuel and Jane Goodson. That was painted in the early 1700s."

"Wow! You're fortunate to have it." He moved on to another picture, this time a large sepia photograph in a wide tortoise-shell frame.

"My grandparents, Andrew and Sophia Goodson," Anna offered.

On the long narrow table beneath Andrew and Sophia's likenesses were a number of smaller, more modern pictures. Anna described each. There were pictures of her parents on their wedding day, and of Anna and her husband, George, on theirs, and pictures of Anna and George's children.

Travis learned that George had died five years earlier, suddenly, of a stroke. All their children were grown and moved away.

It should be like this with Ellie and me, Travis thought. Part of a long line of families blending together through time, pictures scattered about their home of their parents and grandparents and their children and, one day, their grandchildren.

Goosebumps ran up his arms. Grandchildren. Corey's children. Hard to imagine the little boy with the golden curls and chubby cheeks as a man, a father.

It was new to Travis, this sense of his place in the order of life, in its continuity. He liked it. There was a stabilizing feeling to it.

Or there would be, if he and Ellie and Corey were together as a family.

Baby steps, he reminded himself.

He glanced at his watch, wondering what was keeping Chuck. Restless, he wandered back over to Anna and sank onto a huge, round, leather ottoman.

"You're thinking about Ellie, aren't you?" Anna's question was asked in her low, gentle voice, her gaze on her flying fingers and the tan raffia. "You're wondering whether you'll ever be together again."

Travis rested his elbows on his knees and his chin on his

folded hands. "Am I that easy to read?"

Anna only smiled.

"How long were you and George married?"

"Fifty-five years."

"Were you happy?"

"Very. He was more than a man to whom I was legally bound. We loved each other. We were best friends."

It was a gift, Travis realized, to find that kind of love and have all those years to share it. "I suppose Ellie has told you about us, why she left, I mean."

Anna nodded. "She's confided in me, yes."

"Did you and George ever have any problems like that to get past?"

"Problems, yes. Some that seemed mighty large at the time. None that were like yours, no."

He dropped his hands between his knees. "I didn't do it, you know," he said quietly. "Cheat on her, that is. I know it sounds like I did, but I didn't."

Anna didn't respond.

"You don't believe me?"

"I think I do, but it doesn't matter what I believe, does it?"

Travis pushed his hands through his hair and sighed. "I've gone over the months before our breakup a thousand times in my mind, trying to figure out how we reached the place where we were so far apart we could hurt each other as deeply as we did."

"What were the places you stopped listening to each other? George and I found those were the places we needed most to hear each other, the places we needed to grow together, toward each other and forward together." She shrugged her fragile shoulders beneath her soft pink sweater. "Maybe it's not the same for you and Ellie."

Maybe, maybe not. He'd have to think about it.

"One thing I'm sure is true for everyone," Anna continued. "I believe that everything that happens to us is another opportunity to learn to love more like Christ."

"Do you have any advice for me, any wisdom of the ages on how to regain Ellie's trust?"

Anna's hands stilled. She looked directly into Travis's eyes. "How much do you love Ellie and Corey?"

He spread his hands. "More than anything. I've given up my law practice and friends in Los Angeles and moved across the country to be close to them. I've told Ellie I want us to live together like a normal family. I'm giving Ellie money for Corey and setting more aside for his future."

"That's a good start."

"A good start?" Frustration washed through him. What more could a man do than he had already done?

"Is your greatest desire to be together with Ellie and Corey at any cost? Or is it for their lives to be filled with happiness, with God's best for them?"

"Aren't they the same thing? Ellie and I are married. The Bible tells us God doesn't care much for divorce. Doesn't that mean His best is for us to be together as a family?"

Anna went back to her crocheting. "Very likely His perfect will includes the three of you living together as a family and acting in pure love toward each other."

Travis shook his head. One corner of his mouth lifted in a wry grin. "Why does that sound straightforward, but feel like a puzzle?"

Anna only smiled her mysterious, gentle, wise smile.

A strong knock at the door jerked Travis out of his reflective mood and back into the role of protector. "That must be Chuck."

He approved of the dead bolt locks Chuck brought. "Do you have time to install them now?"

"I'll make the time," Chuck replied grimly.

"Have you been in Ellie's house? Do you happen to know what kind of locks she has?"

"Dead bolts. I installed them."

Was that challenge he saw in Chuck's eyes before the carpenter turned away?

Travis wondered about the look as he walked back to the office. He'd noticed the way Chuck had looked at him and Ellie at the shop earlier, too, when Travis had his arm around Ellie, a look of surprise mingled with distaste. Travis hadn't thought much about it at the time. His attention had been on Dan and Jessica.

Uneasiness vined through his chest. Was Chuck interested in Ellie? Were they perhaps seeing each other? She'd told him she wasn't seeing anyone, but Chuck seemed to be around quite a bit. Was he hoping to be next in line in case Ellie filed for divorce?

Travis tried to push the ugly thought away. He couldn't do anything about other men in Ellie's life. He could only concentrate on loving Ellie himself, in whatever ways she'd let him.

Anna's questions skated through his mind. *How much do you love Ellie and Corey? Is your greatest desire to be together with Ellie and Corey at any cost? Or is it for their lives to be filled with happiness, with God's best for them?*

He wanted to spend his life with Ellie and Corey so deeply the ache for that life seemed part of his bones, but he couldn't make that happen.

"I don't have to wait until we're living together to love them," he spoke fiercely into the mountain winds. He knew suddenly and in a deep sense that his love wasn't to be given only in the hope of winning these two precious souls into his home and his arms.

The realization terrified him so much he stopped in his tracks. He started forward again slowly, exploring the new and troubling thought. Amazed, he found that along with the fright he felt freedom; freedom to be vulnerable and love Ellie and Corey completely.

Show me how to love them, Lord, he begged. *Show me how to love them the way You love them, how to be a blessing to them whether or not we ever live together as a family.*

eight

Ellie stopped on the sidewalk in front of Travis's office, hugged the package wrapped in mauve and blue marbled paper to her chest, and took a deep breath. She'd never been to his office. For some reason she couldn't understand, visiting him in his new professional home seemed an acknowledgment that he was here in Blackberry and her life for good.

Still, today was his open house. The remodeling was completed, and Travis was ready to show off his office to the community. She thought it only right that her gift be part of his office.

"Quit stalling," she admonished herself. Straightening her shoulders and lifting her chin, she reached for the door of the old brick building with the new interior. The skirt of her gently shaped pale peach corduroy dress brushed against her calves as she slipped inside.

Ellie entered directly into a large reception area. It looked very contemporary with stained wood timbers bordering white walls and the high white ceiling. She recognized the work of local artists in the wooden tables and lamps, in the pottery decorating the bookcases, and in the Native American pictures by her favorite Cherokee artist on the walls. The earthen colors in the artwork were perfect for the room.

Plants and bouquets were on the tables, bookcases, and floor. Ellie guessed most were gifts from local businesses congratulating Travis on joining their business community.

A middle-aged woman with a professional manner and gray hair cut in a short, contemporary style looked up with a smile from the one desk in the room. "May I help you?"

"I'd like to see Travis, please. Mr. Carter, that is, if he's free." Ellie was surprised she didn't recognize the woman. She knew almost everyone in Blackberry. The name plate on the desk said Mrs. Susan Northrup.

"I'll ask whether he has time to speak with you. Who should I tell him is here?"

"Ellie."

Mrs. Northrup hesitated. "Ellie. . .?"

Ellie flushed. Obviously the receptionist didn't know she was Travis's wife. Ellie wasn't inclined to inform her. "He'll know who I am."

Mrs. Northrup pressed a button on the phone. "Mr. Carter, a young woman named Ellie would like to speak with you if you have a moment."

Ellie started at Travis's voice over the speaker phone. "I'll take the call."

"She is in the office, Mr. Carter."

A moment later the door behind the desk was flung open and Travis strode out to greet Ellie with a huge smile. "This is a pleasant surprise."

"I hope I'm not taking you away from anything urgent."

"Not at all. I haven't any court dates today, and I asked Mrs. Northrup not to schedule any appointments for me in case any last-minute things came up with the remodeling. I needn't have worried. Chuck and the men he hired to help him finished up two days ago."

"It looks great."

"I'll give you a tour." He took her elbow. The simple action sent shivers down Ellie's spine. "First, let me introduce you to my secretary. Mrs. Northrup, this is Ellie Carter. Ellie, Susan Northrup."

Mrs. Northrup's eyes widened slightly at Ellie's last name, but she gave no other indication of her curiosity. The women smiled and nodded at each other as Travis continued. "Any time Ellie calls or stops by, you are to let me know immediately."

"Yes, Mr. Carter."

Ellie indicated the walls and bookshelves with a wave of her palm, freeing herself from Travis's hold at the same time.

"I like what you've done in this room. You chose your art-work well."

"I followed your lead, using local artisans as much as possible as you do with the boutique. I think it's important people in a community support each others' business in art as well as the professions and retail stores. Besides," he flashed a smile, "I genuinely admire the work of the artists represented here."

His appreciation of the talent of the people among whom she'd been raised warmed Ellie's heart, and she returned his smile. "I do, too."

He led her down a hallway off one side of the reception area. Even here his dedication to local artists continued, with photographs of mountain scenes by an award-winning photographer lining the walls, and a runner on the floor by a local weaver.

The last room he showed her was his office. Ellie stood in the middle of the room, her package still clutched to her chest, and looked around. The room was almost as large as the reception area, and decorated in the same manner. A frieze of Native American design topped the wall behind Travis's immense desk.

Everywhere she looked, Ellie saw dollar signs. She knew how much it had cost her to make the simple renovations necessary for the boutique, and how much money was tied up in her inventory, how much she had outstanding in business loans. "The company must think the opportunity for growth is large in this area to invest so much in your office."

"Lots of wealthy men and women retire to this area of the mountains and still need legal advice, even though they've left their business worlds behind them. There's lots of investment going on in these hills, too. The firm is hoping its reputation in the Piedmont will bring clients familiar with the name through our doors. They want the office here to represent the firm's successful image."

"I'm sure it will do that." Obviously he still liked the money and prestige of a large firm. He wasn't the village type.

"Have you and Jessica had any trouble with Dan lately?"

"No. Jessica is on pins and needles every other weekend when Brent goes to stay with Dan. She's afraid one of these times Brent is going to come home with bruises, if not broken bones."

"It's a valid fear." Travis's comment was grim. "She told me he hasn't made any threats since the incident at the boutique, but I wasn't sure she was being honest with me."

"She hasn't told me about any more threats. I expect the old ones are still good."

Travis grimaced.

"Thank you for offering her free legal advice. I know she's talked with you about the situation with Dan."

"There's not much I can do to help her at this point. Are you two remembering to keep your house locked?"

"Yes." Now it was Ellie's turn to grimace. "We're beginning to feel like prisoners."

A wooden carving on the edge of his desk of a Cherokee man, woman, and child caught her attention. The woman was looking over her shoulder, sadness in every line of her face. Ellie reached out and ran a finger lightly over the wooden cheek. She felt as though she wanted to wipe away a tear the artist hadn't put there, but whose presence could still be felt. "I haven't seen this artist's work before. It's magnificent."

"I bought it from the artist at his shop near Cherokee. He told me it's of a family just starting out on the Trail of Tears." He cleared his throat and shrugged his shoulders, looking a little embarrassed. "I haven't had it long. Still chokes me up to look at it."

Ellie could understand that. She liked him all the more for allowing himself to feel the emotion of this family's story, of the Cherokees' story.

"Makes me think we have life pretty easy." Travis was looking at the carving. "The thought of being forced to start out on a journey like that into the unknown with Corey—" He shivered. "It's terrifying."

"Yes." More terrifying than when she'd first told Travis about Corey and wondered whether he'd try to take the boy away from her. She was convinced now that he wouldn't do that, but she was still not ready to trust him to stay faithful to their marriage vows.

"Sit down." Travis waved her toward the pair of leather wing chairs facing his desk.

"I can't stay."

"I've been so busy showing off the office that I didn't think to ask why you stopped. Is it a legal matter?"

"No." She held out the package. "I thought you might like this for your desk."

His face lit up like a kid's at Christmas. He tore the paper away. Emotions chased across his face like clouds across a sky: disbelief, gratitude, joy.

"I thought you should have a picture of your son for your office." It was a framed eight-by-twelve print of the wallet-sized photo she'd sent him months earlier. "It's the most recent professional shot I have of him. He's changed quite a bit since it was taken, but—"

"It's perfect." His husky assurance stopped her excuses. "It's perfect. Thank you."

Ellie took a couple of steps backward toward the door, glad Travis's desk was between them. The way he was looking at her, his heart in his eyes, made her ache to be in his arms. She moistened her suddenly dry lips with the tip of her tongue. "I'd better be getting back to the boutique."

"You're welcome to stay for the open house, or come back for it. It starts in an hour." He set the picture in a prominent place on his desk, ran his hand caressingly across the top of the cherry frame, and started toward her.

"I don't know if I can get away from the shop again today." Too many townspeople knew she and Travis were married. She didn't want people to think they were more of a family than they were in fact. If she were here during an important event like his open house, people might think they'd reconciled.

Maybe Travis would take it as a sign she wanted to reconcile. She wasn't ready for that yet.

What made her tack *yet* on the end of that thought? Dismay twisted her stomach into knots. Was it possible her heart wanted to let him back into a real marriage, under one roof and in one bed? Or was it hormones speaking and not her heart?

Travis had been altogether too appealing since moving here. In spite of the hours involved in getting his office and business up and going, he made sure he saw Corey every day. He'd been faithful to his promise to provide a weekly check to help with Corey's financial support. He hadn't pressured her any more to get together. She was beginning to feel almost relaxed around him, at least most of the time. It was plain he enjoyed the time he spent with her and Corey. But she didn't dare let herself trust him.

In the reception area she saw a long table had been set up along one wall. Mrs. Northrup was straightening a white tablecloth.

Anna came from the hallway with a tray of chicken salad on bite-size buns. Her wrinkled face broke into a sunny smile when she recognized Ellie. "Are you here to help with the open house, too?"

"No." Ellie shook her head vehemently.

Anna set the tray down. "I'm so excited that Travis asked me to help serve the refreshments and greet guests. He insisted on buying me a new dress. I bought it at your shop, of course. Jessica helped me pick it out. What do you think?" She spread her arms wide and turned about like a little girl.

The dress was a total departure from Anna's usual traditional lace-trimmed pastels. It was a sunlit chestnut brown with a crinkle skirt of fluid rayon challis and matching blouse with a small Native American design in black on the collar and placket. A matching embroidered vest added an elegant touch. A braided leather belt with a round silver buckle completed the ensemble. Ellie recognized Jessica's handiwork in the rectangular silver earrings and pin with a jack-in-the-pulpit design.

"You look spectacular," Ellie told Anna sincerely, squeezing the older woman's hands.

"I feel brand new," Anna confided in a loud whisper.

"I hope you're the same old Anna underneath," Ellie teased, "but the new style looks good on you."

"I'm glad you think so, since you designed it."

Travis followed her out of the building. "Ellie, I was wondering if we could go to church together this Sunday, you and me and Corey."

Like a family. Ellie shivered. "I. . .I don't think so, no. I hope your open house goes well." She turned on her heel and hurried off before he could press her further.

Conflicting emotions tumbled through her heart and conflicting thoughts through her mind as she headed toward the boutique. She wished the spring breeze could blow away the fog of confusion concerning her feelings for Travis. Should she trust him or shouldn't she? The chant went on day after day. It was fatiguing her.

She greeted townspeople along her way with absentminded smiles. How many of them would be attending Travis's open house? The town had taken him to its heart in the short time he'd been here. He'd accepted the church's request to join the board. He met with other businessmen over lunch and dinner in the local restaurants. He attended the weekly prayer breakfasts. Even Mr. Hobson, the elderly gentleman who had been the village's primary lawyer all his professional life, had told her Travis was an asset to the community. Everyone but Ellie seemed smitten with Travis.

Maybe not everyone. She suspected Dan didn't care for Travis one bit.

"I wish I could trust him completely," she whispered into the spring air. She was tired of worrying whether she had been right to let him back into Corey's life, tired of worrying whether Travis might hurt her again, tired of trying to deny her enjoyment of his company, tired of fighting her desire to be in his arms again.

I wish it could be one way or the other, she told the Lord silently. *I wish he was out of our lives completely or in our lives completely. Trying to balance between friendship and intimacy is like walking along the top of a picket fence.*

Ellie shivered and hugged her arms. *How long before I lose my balance and fall off?*

❧

That evening Ellie and Jess had sloppy joes and potato chips for supper. It was one of the boys' favorite meals. Jess always liked to make sure Brent's time was pleasant right before Dan picked the boy up for a weekend.

Ellie watched the boys giggling as they ate, finding typical little-boy humor in the way the meat and sauce were dripping from the sandwiches, dribbling from chins, and tumbling down the fronts of their T-shirts. She and Jessica had given up trying to convince the boys to wear bibs on sloppy joe nights. Corey and Brent insisted they were too old for bibs. Their mothers gave in, and instead of bibs allowed the boys to wear their oldest T-shirts.

Ellie knew Jessica had a clean shirt ready to put on Brent as soon as he was done eating. Neither of the women liked the boys running around in clothes covered with food, but the sight made Dan livid.

Jessica glanced at the clock, grimaced, and shifted her weight.

Ellie checked the time. Almost seven. Dan would be here any minute. Her stomach tightened in the familiar response to Dan's imminent arrival. She set down her own sandwich. She couldn't eat it now.

But when she answered the door a few minutes later, with the sound of Jessica's voice hurrying Brent to finish eating in the background, it wasn't Dan who entered but Travis.

She looked at him in surprise. "I wasn't expecting you. Did we agree you'd see Corey tonight? If so, I forgot."

"No. Jess stopped at the open house. She was upset about Dan picking Brent up for the weekend." He shrugged. "I thought if I was here when Dan arrived, things might go smoother."

"I'm not sure it will make any difference. Dan is never actually violent when he picks up Brent. It's the boys who get upset, not wanting Brent to leave. And Jessica gets upset worrying what might happen to Brent while he's with Dan."

Travis raised his eyebrows in question marks. "So this was a dumb idea?"

"It was a kind gesture, and maybe your presence will make Jessica feel better." She waved a hand toward the kitchen. "The boys are eating. You can go in and say hello if you'd like."

"Dinner smells good." He raised his face as if sniffing the air. "I came directly from the office. All I've eaten today are the cookies and minuscule sandwiches Anna and Mrs. Northrup provided for the open house."

Ellie laughed. "If that's a hint that your man-size stomach is growling, you're welcome to have a sloppy joe with the boys."

"Thanks." He headed down the hall, sliding his coat off as he went.

Ellie leaned against the kitchen wall with her arms crossed over her coppery chenille sweater and watched Travis and the boys.

As usual, Corey and Brent were delighted to see Travis. He'd barely sat down when he commented on the blobs of sloppy joe that decorated the boys' shirts. "Don't you think you need bibs?"

They shook their heads vigorously.

Travis looked down at his white shirt. "Think I need one. Do you have one that will fit me?"

The boys burst into giggles.

Ellie smiled. She could never help smiling when the boys giggled in the full-fledged manner that jiggled their entire little bodies and shined from their eyes.

"No," Corey managed to force out in between the giggles.

"No?" Travis looked crestfallen.

Corey shook his head, his giggles diminishing.

"Guess I'll need to use this then." Travis stuck a napkin in his collar.

It set the boys into stitches again.

Warmth filled Ellie's chest. It took so little to bring joy to the boys. All they wanted was a few minutes of uncritical, undivided attention.

The doorbell's ring brought Ellie out of her reverie. As she hurried to answer it, the bell rang again and again, pushing away the comfortable, warm moment. She pressed her lips together in irritation and yanked open the door.

Dan entered without an invitation. Annoyance filled his eyes. His hands were plunged into the pockets of the lined trench coat he always wore. He didn't bother with a friendly preamble. "Where's Brent?"

"He's just finishing supper." Jessica spoke from the kitchen doorway.

Dan's mouth tightened. "Why isn't he done? You knew I'd be here at seven."

Ellie could see Jessica working to control her temper and knew she was afraid if she said what she felt, Dan would take his anger at her out on Brent later.

"Sorry," Jessica apologized, "he's almost done."

"Get him out here. I want to get going."

Ellie wondered what he could possibly have planned for the evening that would be ruined if he waited for Brent to finish eating, but she didn't ask.

"Let him finish his sandwich," Jessica asked reasonably.

Dan flashed her an impatient look. "If you won't get him, I will." He started for the kitchen.

He stopped abruptly inside the kitchen door.

Behind him Ellie saw the satisfaction in Jessica's face at Dan's surprise and knew she was glad Travis was there. A gloating sense of satisfaction filled Ellie, too.

Travis looked up calmly. "Hello, Dan. Going to join us?"

Dan hesitated, obviously put off by Travis's unexpected presence and friendly gesture.

The boys had stopped eating and were watching Dan warily.

Dan strode toward Brent. "Get your coat on."

"The boy hasn't finished his dinner." Travis's quiet but firm tone made the simple words a threat.

His hand on Brent's shoulder, Dan threw an uneasy glance at Travis.

Without standing up, Travis drew out a chair. Its legs squeaked across the linoleum. "Why don't you sit down and join us?"

Dan ignored the chair. "Hurry up and finish eating."

Brent obediently took another bite.

Ellie could have cried at the boy's forlorn face.

"Thanks for stopping by the open house today, Dan." Travis's voice and face revealed nothing of what he might be feeling. "And for the plant you sent."

Dan grunted something that might have been "You're welcome" and finally dropped into the chair. "Nice office."

Ellie could hear the envy in Dan's voice. His office, though nice, didn't begin to compare to Travis's, but Dan didn't have a large regional firm behind him like Travis did. She was surprised Dan had sent a plant to the open house, let alone shown up. Probably he only did so because he thought it was expected by the rest of the business community. The open house was a good place to network.

After only two bites, Brent set his sandwich down. "I don't want any more."

"Are you sure, honey?" Jessica leaned over him. "You haven't eaten much. Maybe you'd like to take it along with you."

"No," Dan exploded. "He's not going to eat in my car."

Ellie grinned at the vision of tomato sauce spotting the interior of his Mercedes.

Jessica evidently had no such cheering vision. "Do you have

anything to feed Brent if he's hungry later?" she asked Dan.

"Of course, I do." Belligerency drenched his words.

Ellie wondered, as she was sure Jessica did, whether Brent would have the courage if he was hungry to ask Dan for food.

Dan scowled. "Don't you have a clean shirt for him, Jessie? He's a mess. I don't know why you don't make him wear a bib since he's not grown up enough to eat like a man."

Brent's mouth turned down at the corners, and he climbed off his chair.

Corey stared wide-eyed at Dan.

Ellie was glad her son apparently knew instinctively that this was a man who could not be trusted.

Travis deliberately wiped his mouth with the napkin still stuck in his collar. He winked at Brent and grinned. "Next time we have sloppy joes, you and Corey can wear a man-sized napkin like mine."

Brent rewarded Travis with a smile, though it wasn't a wholehearted one.

Jessica took Brent's hand. "Come on, honey, let's change your shirt."

"Hurry it up." Dan scraped back his chair. "I haven't got all night."

While Jessica was changing Brent, Ellie wrapped a couple of chocolate chip cookies in a napkin.

She collected Brent's jacket and gloves, surreptitiously sticking the cookies into a jacket pocket before handing it to Jessica.

Travis, who was standing with Corey in his arms in the kitchen doorway, winked at Ellie.

She allowed herself a small smile back, one that wouldn't catch Dan's attention.

Corey's arm was about Travis's neck. Ellie hated the resignation in Corey's wide-eyed gaze. He always hated to see his friend head off for the weekend.

Jessica pulled a billed blue corduroy hat over Brent's forehead and gave him a big hug. "I love you, Brent."

Brent clung to her.

Ellie blinked back tears as Jessica gently but firmly removed her arms. Tears shone in Jessica's eyes, too.

"You'll make sure Brent is dressed warmly if you take him outside, won't you?" Jessica asked Dan as she stood up.

"Of course. Think I'm some kind of moron?" Dan lifted Brent's red and blue duffle bag.

Ellie knelt down and surrounded Brent with her arms. "I love you, sweetheart."

"'Bye, partner," Travis said.

Brent waved forlornly at Travis and Corey.

Dan reached for Brent's hand.

Brent extended his reluctantly. "Can Corey come?" His gaze sought his friend.

"No." Dan tugged at Brent's hand.

The boy followed along with his father for a couple of steps. At the door he looked back over his shoulder. "I don' wanna go, Momma!" His face crumpled into tears.

"Don't be a baby." Dan scooped the boy into his arms and headed out the door before Jessica had a chance to reply.

Jessica sank to the bottom step of the hall stairs and dropped her face into her hands. Her shoulders shook with quiet sobs.

Corey stared at her and hugged Travis's neck.

Travis's face was a study in controlled fury.

Ellie darted out the door. She reached Dan and Brent at the open back car door. Brent was climbing into his car seat.

In the front seat was Sissy Barr, a young woman Ellie recognized as having graduated from high school only two years ago. This, then, was the reason Dan was in even more of a hurry than usual. The girl wiggled her fingers at Ellie in a wave.

Dan looked at Ellie in surprise. "Did I forget something?"

"No. I did. I forgot to tell you that I'm not afraid of you like Jessica is. You better watch Brent very carefully and hope he doesn't fall down or run into anything. If he comes back with so much as a penny-sized bruise, I'll tell the sheriff what you've done to Jessica in the past."

Dan's eyes were black with rage. "I've never laid a hand on Jessie."

She ignored his protest. "I promise you I'm not going to let you get away with hurting this boy. He's a treasure."

Dan leaned into the car and fastened Brent's car-seat belt, then slammed the car door. Glaring at her, he climbed into the front seat, turned on the ignition, and closed the door.

Ellie smiled and waved at Brent as the car started to back out of the driveway.

Turning back to the house, she saw Travis, Corey, and Jessica standing in the doorway. Ellie caught back a groan and smiled as she walked toward them, shivering in the early spring evening.

"What did you say to him?" Jessica asked, closing the door behind Ellie.

Ellie shrugged. "Just wanted to say another good-bye to Brent."

Jessica eyed her suspiciously but didn't push it.

Ellie gave her a hug. "You doing okay?"

Jessica nodded, but her face was still flushed and her eyes red from the tears she'd shed. "Why don't I do the dishes while you guys visit?"

"I can help," Ellie offered.

"No. I. . .I'd like to spend a few minutes alone. Might as well spend them doing something worthwhile." Jessica stopped just outside the kitchen door and turned to Travis with a small smile. "Thanks for coming."

"Sure."

Travis, Corey, and Ellie wandered into the living room. Corey wiggled to be let down, and Travis obliged. The boy went to the TV stand, picked up a video tape, and brought it to Ellie. Ellie rolled her eyes.

"What is it?" Travis took the tape from her and scowled down at it. "Teletubbies?"

Ellie nodded. "A Teletubbies movie. It's his favorite video. We've seen it so many times I've lost count."

"Put it in," Corey demanded, pointing to the TV.

Ellie nodded in response to Travis's questioning look. "We might as well. Maybe it will take his mind off his little friend for awhile."

Travis stuck the tape into the recorder. Corey picked up the gray horse which had been Travis's first gift. The boy hugged it to him as he sat down in front of the television.

Travis picked up a small book with a red leather cover from the end table beside the sofa. "*In His Steps*. I've heard of this. Are you reading it?"

"Yes. Rereading it actually."

Travis riffled the pages and set it back down.

Ellie sat on the sofa, dropping her head against the back. "I feel like I've been through a war."

Travis dropped down beside her. He leaned close, speaking low, glancing at Corey. "Is it always this way when Dan picks up Brent?"

"Oh, no. Sometimes it's worse. I think it did help that you were here. Brent hates spending weekends with Dan. Knowing it sets Dan off."

"Something should be done to prevent it then."

"You're the lawyer. You know how hard it is to keep a father from his children. Besides, the separation agreement says Brent will spend every other weekend with Dan."

"If I didn't know the law, I don't think I would have allowed Dan to take Brent out of here tonight. It was all I could do not to grab that boy and hold on for dear life."

Ellie's chest flooded with admiration. Regardless of anything else she might feel for this man, she loved the way he loved Corey and Brent.

A muscle jumped in Travis's cheek. "I wanted to wallop the guy."

"I know the feeling." She sighed and brushed back her hair. "So much for walking in Christ's footsteps."

"Wanting to protect the boy has to be a Christ-inspired desire. Knowing how to go about it in a Christ-centered way, that's the difficult part."

"Yes." She studied his face thoughtfully. It was only a few inches away, as they were still trying to prevent Corey from overhearing their conversation.

Travis slid down a bit so he could rest his head against the back of the sofa, too. His shoulder pressed against Ellie's. The hint of intimacy in the simple touch filled her stomach with butterflies. Was it playing with fire, sitting with him like this, with Corey in the same room watching television, acting like a family?

"I don't get it." Travis's gaze was on Corey. "Dan doesn't seem to even like Brent."

"I know." She told him about the girl in Dan's car. "I wonder how much attention Brent will receive from Dan tonight with Sissy around."

"Why does Dan want to spend every other weekend with the boy when he doesn't like having him around?"

"To hurt Jessica."

Travis turned his head to face her. "He hates her that much?"

"He says he loves her, but love doesn't act that way."

"Love doesn't. Wounds do."

Ellie studied Travis's eyes, thinking about his words. She wasn't sure she agreed with him. There was only acting from love and not acting from love, wasn't there? Was there ever an excuse to choose to not act from love?

Her conscience made her squirm inside. Had she acted in love when she left Travis? Hadn't her actions resulted from her wounds? She'd defended her actions ever since by saying she'd been protecting herself from being hurt again. Her excuses had since grown to protecting Corey, too.

She'd think about it later. Maybe. Right now it was more comfortable to talk about Dan and Jessica. "I think it hurt Dan's ego when Jessica left, not his heart. Now he's trying to pay her back."

"He's doing it all too well."

"Yes," she whispered, remembering the pain in her friend's eyes and in Brent's, "but it's his own fault she left. If he hadn't hit her, she'd have stayed with him."

Pain shot through Travis's eyes. "I know."

Was Travis thinking that it was his own fault that she had left him, too? Ellie wondered. Travis thought it all right for Jessica to leave a man for causing her physical harm. What did he think about Ellie leaving him because he'd caused her emotional harm?

She wasn't about to ask. Her thoughts went around in the familiar circle. She wasn't sure how she felt about it herself. All she knew was that she didn't want Corey to experience the betrayal she'd felt and she didn't want to experience it again, either.

Travis's hand enveloped hers. She shifted her glance from his eyes to their joined hands. His thumb played lightly over the back of her hand, sending delightful shivers down her spine and wonderful memories echoing through her mind.

"I'm sorry, Ellie."

Her gaze darted back to his eyes, but now he was watching their hands.

"I'm sorry I hurt you so much." His husky whisper cracked on the words.

She wanted to say it was all right. She wanted to tell him she believed him. She wanted to tell him she still loved him. She wanted to tell him how much she missed being in his arms. She wanted to tell him she was sorry she'd hurt him, too. She wanted to tell him how glad she was they saw each other every day, and she knew he was all right. She wanted to tell him how much she loved seeing him and Corey together.

She wanted to never doubt him again, for her sake and for Corey's. But she did doubt him. A piece of her couldn't let go of the fear he'd betray her again.

Still, she left her hand in his, remembering the beauty of his touch when her trust in him had been complete. Her shoulder continued to rest comfortably against his. Their heads remained so close together she could feel his breath.

"Let Co'ey up."

Ellie and Travis started at Corey's demand.

Corey shoved his stuffed horse into their hands. "Up."

Chuckling, Travis settled the boy on his lap. Corey wasn't content. He tried wiggling in between Travis and Ellie. They got the message and moved to allow him room.

Travis slipped an arm over Corey's shoulders, and Corey leaned back, content written wide on his face. "Look." He pointed toward the television where the Teletubbies were tumbling about.

Ellie smiled as Travis made some appropriate noises of appreciation.

Travis pointed out different Teletubbies. He looked delighted when Corey was able to name each one.

"Think your mom will let us have some of those chocolate chip cookies that are out in the kitchen?" Travis asked Corey.

Corey nodded. "Mom, can we have cookies?"

"I'll bring you some. Do you want a glass of milk, too, Corey?"

Corey nodded. "Uh-huh."

Ellie smiled mischievously at Travis. "How about you, milk or coffee?"

He met her mischievous smile with one of his own. "Do I have any other choices? Besides beverages, I mean."

His meaning wasn't lost on her. The old phrase "coffee, tea, or me" jumped into her mind, sending heat racing to her cheeks and her feet heading for the kitchen.

At the entry to the hallway she glanced back at the two men in her life and smiled. Already Corey had Travis's undivided attention again.

Reluctantly she left her view of them for the kitchen. The sight of them together always made her feel downright mushy. Would the three of them ever be together like this as a family in every sense of the word?

nine

Ellie hummed as she went about her work Monday. Sunny, warm spring weather was bringing tourists from the Piedmont into the mountains and into her store. Her spring line was selling well.

The cash register provided background music for the brass bells above the door, until Ellie decided to keep the door open. The air carried in fragrances of spring blossoms and grasses, a pleasant change from the potpourris which scented the shop in the winter months.

"There should be spring tunes blaring from loudspeakers today the way Christmas carols do in December," she told Anna with a laugh.

"Easter hymns would be nice."

A thirty-ish woman with a red pageboy stepped into the shop about noon. Ellie eyed the woman with curiosity. She was dressed in a lovely designer suit, not typical tourist attire. Ellie wondered if the woman was a new professional in town.

She was examining a pale blue linen suit when Ellie approached her. Expensive perfume overpowered the spring scents. "May I help you find something?"

The woman's face brightened. "You must be Ellie Carter."

"Yes." She always felt uncomfortable when people she didn't know recognized her.

"I recognized you from Travis's description." The woman held out a hand. "I'm Angie Adams."

Ellie met Angie's hand with her own, though dread and caution were winding through Ellie's breast. How well did Travis and Angie Adams know each other? She wanted to ask how they'd met, but chose not to. Ellie wasn't about to let this woman she'd just met know it mattered to her one iota what women Travis knew. "Do you live in Blackberry?"

"Oh, my, no." Angie gave a dismissing little wave with a finely manicured hand. Ellie noticed there were no wedding or engagement rings on it. "I'm from the law firm's Charlotte office. I'll be helping Travis out on a case."

"I see." Ellie's dread lifted somewhat but not totally. "I hope you'll like our village."

"It's charming." Angie leaned toward Ellie in a confidential manner that made Ellie want to back away. "Travis offered to take me to lunch today, the way people in the firm always do when someone from one of the other offices is working with them. I turned him down because he told me about your shop. I knew I had to visit it first thing."

"How kind of you," Ellie murmured.

"He raved about your talent as a designer. Positively raved." Angie flipped her hand in the annoying waving motion again.

"He did?" Surprise and pleasure surged through Ellie like a dancing mountain creek.

"Raved," Angie assured her, widening her green eyes and leaning even closer to emphasize her point.

"How nice." Ellie tried not to beam on the outside the way she was on the inside. It might be springtime, but she felt like a Christmas tree in full dress and brilliantly lit.

She wondered whether Travis had told Angie that he was married to Ellie and, if so, whether he'd told Angie he was separated. She wasn't about to offer the information herself.

When Angie left the shop forty-five minutes later, she was carrying the blue linen suit and was assuring Ellie that Travis had been right about her designs and promising she would return another day. "We simply must do lunch while I'm in town."

Ellie waited until Angie had passed the shop windows, then looked at Anna. The older woman's blue eyes were dancing. A moment later both women burst into laughter.

"Can you imagine that woman in court?" Ellie asked when she could breathe again. "She looks the perfect professional, but her mannerisms. . . ." Ellie couldn't find the words. "Judges probably rule in her favor just to get her to stop talking."

"Or to get her perfume out of their courtrooms."

They broke into giggles again.

Ellie dabbed at the corner of her eye to catch a laughter tear. "I suppose that was catty of us. She was nice enough. She didn't have to buy that suit, or even stop at the shop or tell me Travis had complimented my designs."

"Or gush over the lace collar I made for the suit she bought." Anna lifted her white blouse's peter-pan collar and pretended to preen.

"I was a little afraid. . .a lot afraid. . .when she told me she was working with Travis." It was hard to admit, even to Anna, in whom Ellie had confided so much.

Anna patted her hand. "That's only natural, dear."

"Do you know Travis's receptionist, Susan Northrup? I didn't recognize her when I met her at his office the other day, and I thought I knew everyone in town."

Anna brightened. "Oh, yes, I know her. Her oldest sister is a friend of mine. Susan and her husband live in Blowing Rock."

"Why did he hire someone who lives over thirty miles away? I would think he could have found a receptionist and secretary who lived closer."

"A couple of young women applied. He wanted someone more mature. He was afraid if he put that in the ad or told the employment agency that he'd be accused of reverse age discrimination." Anna chuckled, her soft rosy cheeks wrinkling pleasantly.

Ellie smiled with her. "Did he think someone older would be more experienced?"

"Not necessarily." Anna hesitated, fingering her collar. "He thought you would be more comfortable if his secretary were older."

"Me?"

"Yes. He didn't want to give you any reason to be. . .suspicious. . .that there might be something improper going on between him and his employee."

Ellie stared at her, amazed Travis had given a moment's thought to his wife's reaction to whom he hired.

"He says he wasn't unfaithful to you with that woman in Los Angeles," Anna said quietly. "You do know that, don't you?"

"I know." Ellie's lips were suddenly stiff. She knew he'd said that he wasn't unfaithful, but she also knew what she'd seen and heard.

She was spared expanding on her thoughts to Anna by Chuck's arrival.

He greeted them cheerfully, leaned his elbows on the counter, shoved up the bill of his ever-present baseball hat, and grinned at Ellie. "Have you had lunch yet? I'd be glad to treat at the Black Bear."

"Thanks, but I can't make it today. Anna will be heading home any minute. Jessica has been watching the boys this morning while she worked on some jewelry sketches. Anna's going to take over for her for the afternoon, and Jessica's coming down here to help me out."

Ellie was glad Chuck left without appearing too downhearted.

A few minutes after Anna left, Chuck returned with a brown paper bag which emitted the tempting aroma of a Black Bear hamburger and french fries. "Since you won't go to the food, I'm bringing the food to you. You go without lunch all too often."

"Thanks. I didn't realize I was hungry until you walked in with this."

"I brought something for both of us, so you don't have to eat alone."

"We'd better go to the back room." She didn't want customers to see her chomping away on a burger or have the odors she found so tempting to her taste buds assailing her customers in the shop. She didn't want to encourage Chuck, either. Of course, he hadn't crossed the line of friendship yet, but she didn't want him to think she was encouraging him to do so, either. She knew how easy it was for men and women to misinterpret each other's actions.

They ate standing beside the work table where she could see into the shop. Unfortunately for her cash register but fortunately for her digestion, no customers entered the shop while she and Chuck ate.

Conversation between them was easy at first, as it had always been. From the beginning they'd found it easy to be together, sharing many interests and a common sense of humor. They were almost done eating when he told her he'd been to Travis's open house.

"He has a nice office, doesn't he?" she said.

"Yeah."

His almost-surly tone alerted her to a shift in his mood. For a couple of minutes neither of them spoke. She searched her mind for a non-controversial topic and finally told him about Dan picking up Brent at the beginning of the weekend. She even told him about her challenge to Dan in the driveway.

"I assume he returned Brent in good health."

"Yes, in physically good health at least. The way Dan treats the boy has to be taking its toll emotionally."

"I saw Dan Friday night about nine. He was at a movie with Sissy Barr."

"They took Brent to a movie?"

Chuck shook his head. "I didn't see Brent there."

Anger rose in her as quickly as a creek overflowing its banks in a flash flood. Dan had cruelly rushed Brent away from his mother and Corey to leave him with a sitter while he, a married man, went out on a date.

"Didn't Brent tell you?" Chuck asked.

"He's too young to tell us. He might tell us he'd played with the babysitter, but. . ." Dawning realization cut short her thought.

"But what?"

"He didn't mention a babysitter. Maybe. . ." She didn't like what she was thinking. It made her stomach feel like she'd just had a glass of sour milk. "Maybe there wasn't a babysitter."

"Even Dan's not enough of a creep to leave a youngster Brent's size alone." Chuck's eyebrows met above troubled eyes. "Is he?"

Ellie didn't answer. She didn't know the answer.

"Thinkin' of that little guy maybe left alone. . ." Chuck removed his baseball hat and wiped his forehead with his forearm. "Makes my skin crawl."

Neither of them spoke for a couple of minutes, each examining the horrible thought in the privacy of their own minds.

There was nothing to be gained by it, not at the moment. "I'll ask Jessica about the babysitter tonight," Ellie told him. "Maybe Brent said something to Jessica."

"I hope so."

Ellie searched for a more pleasant topic.

"Does Corey miss Brent when he's with Dan?" Chuck asked.

"Yes. We watched a Teletubbies movie with him after Brent left, hoping to divert his attention for awhile." She laughed, and told Chuck about Travis's funny ways with Corey while they watched the movie.

Chuck didn't find them amusing. "Travis spent the evening at your house?"

"He's Corey's father," she reminded him gently. "They need to spend time together."

"Have you told Corey yet that Travis is his father?"

"No."

"Aren't you afraid Travis will tell him before you do?"

She went numb at his question. The possibility hadn't occurred to her. She and Travis had never discussed when and if they would reveal Travis and Corey's relationship to the boy, though she had no intention of telling that to Chuck. "I don't think Travis will do that. Even if he did, I'm not certain Corey is old enough to understand."

"Are you sure?"

She didn't answer. Ellie met his gaze evenly as he studied her eyes.

"Am I prying, Ellie?"

"You've been a good friend to me ever since I moved back to Blackberry, but this part of my life. . .my family, my marriage. . ."

Chuck's jaw tightened. "Have you decided to go back to Travis?"

"No. That is, I don't know. I'm praying about it."

"Don't do it, Ellie."

"Don't pray about it?" she asked, purposely misunderstanding, trying to lighten the emotions between them.

His eyes flashed, but his voice only registered frustration. "Don't go back to Travis. You can't trust him." He crumpled up his sandwich wrapping and tossed it onto the work table. "Once you've let him back into your life and he feels secure, he will hurt you again. Leopards don't change their spots."

"Oh, please." Ellie rolled her eyes. "That's not very original."

"Most sayings that last do so because they have a lot of truth in them."

She knew he was right. It was what she feared most, that leopards didn't change their spots, that Travis hadn't changed his unfaithful ways, either. After all, he'd moved to Blackberry because he'd discovered he had a son. He'd known she'd moved to Blackberry when she left Los Angeles. He'd known how to reach her through her parents if he'd wished. He hadn't. Now that he was here, now that he knew Corey, Travis had told her he'd missed her and wanted to be back together, but was it truly because he loved her, or only because he wanted to live with their son?

Ellie shivered, hating the way the cruel thoughts wormed into her heart and mind and clouded the sunshine of the spring day.

ten

"Say yes, Ellie," Travis begged, keeping his tone light with an effort. "It's going to be a beautiful April afternoon. We should take advantage of it. The forecast is for a snowstorm to move in tonight."

The mountains in springtime couldn't be any more beautiful than Ellie, he thought. She was lovely today as always, wearing a simple light-blue shift with a blue sweater over her shoulders. Sunshine poured through the stained-glass windows, delicately lighting her chestnut hair.

People passed them in the aisle, making their way to the church doors now that the service was over. Many smiled or raised a hand in hello. Travis returned their greetings, liking the way it felt to be part of this church family.

Jessica laid a hand on Ellie's arm. "Go ahead. It will be good for you. You've been working like a slave laborer the last few weeks."

"I hate to leave you with the boys."

"We can take them with us," Travis offered immediately. He and Ellie hadn't spent any time alone since he moved to Blackberry, but if the only way he could get her out on a picnic was with the boys, that was fine with him. "They're always good company."

"I will watch the boys," Jessica informed them in a tone that invited no argument. "Brent spent last weekend with Dan. I'm not giving up my Sunday with my boy. Speaking of the boys, I'll head down to the nursery and round them up." She leaned close to Ellie and said in a stage whisper, "Go. Get out of town. Corey will be fine with me and Brent."

Travis tried again. "Anna promised to send a picnic basket with us. If that doesn't tempt you, nothing will."

Ellie spread her arms and laughed. "All right, I give in. What else can I do with all of you conspiring against me?"

An hour later with the picnic basket in the back of Travis's red Jeep and Ellie and Travis in the front seats, they were headed down the Blue Ridge Parkway. Both had changed from their Sunday finery into jeans, sweatshirts, and short leather boots which would be good for walking mountain trails.

Ellie stretched. "I feel as if I've been kidnaped."

"I promise to return you safely with no ransom demand."

His words brought a lazy laugh from Ellie, but he knew the promise would be harder to keep than she realized. Not that he had any fantasies of a money ransom. Daily trying to love her and Corey the way Anna suggested was difficult; loving them without asking to be loved and trusted in return. That was the ransom that was so hard not to demand: love and trust and a life together under one roof.

He wanted them to be living together and loving each other in a family setting so badly there were times he could hardly bear it. He wanted Ellie the way every man wants the woman he loves. He didn't dare press it.

Baby steps, he reminded himself.

Right now he tried to content himself with sharing one of the most beautiful places in the world with his wife and cheered himself with the reminder that she was still his wife, that in spite of everything, she hadn't divorced him.

They ooohed and aaahed over the views of mountains and valleys as they traveled along. There appeared to be only a few areas of private land along the parkway. Most of the road traveled through natural settings.

"I've been over this drive many times, but I never grow tired of it," Ellie said. "I'm glad you talked me into coming up here today."

His heart ballooned with joy. "I'd take credit for the views if I could. As it is, I'm grateful for the people who set this land apart for a national treasure so many years ago. If they hadn't, it would likely be covered with condominiums, private resorts, and billboards announcing tourist sites."

He pulled to the side and parked where they had a view of a private hillside covered with trees that were a froth of pink blossoms. He rolled down his window and welcomed in their fragrance. "Apple trees?"

"Peach trees. Unfortunately, if the weather forecast is correct, those blossoms will be covered with snow by tomorrow. I hope the farmer doesn't lose his entire crop."

He stared at the rosy-pink beauty, and a little sadness crept over him. "Nature can be cruel."

"Yes." A minute later she amended her response. "Sometimes what seems cruel isn't, or at least it has beautiful benefits. I remember when I was a teenager a bad wind storm toppled hundreds of trees on the mountain behind my parents' home. I felt as devastated as the mountain looked. The next spring, dogwoods and rhododendrons blossomed where the tall trees had stood. The blossoming trees had been there before, of course, but the older trees had shadowed them. Now the smaller trees could reach wide for the sun. I remind myself of that when life is hard." She bit her bottom lip, looking embarrassed. "I guess that sounds hokey."

He shook his head. "No, not a bit."

He hoped that would happen for them; that the storm of separation would pass and leave their life more beautiful. He popped his palms lightly against the steering wheel and took a deep breath, breaking the sentimental spell. "Ready for lunch?"

Travis took the picnic basket and red-and-black plaid blanket from the back of the Jeep. Together he and Ellie spread the blanket on the ground.

"When did you buy the Jeep?" Ellie asked as he opened the picnic basket.

"Last week. I decided sports cars weren't made for mountain living, at least not if you plan to drive them all year."

"You traded your car? You loved that car."

Travis shrugged. "I decided a four-wheel-drive vehicle made more sense."

"Don't tell me you, the citified lawyer, are becoming a red—true mountain man." Her teasing tone kept the statement from sounding like an insult.

He chuckled. "What was that you almost called me? A redneck?"

She tossed her head in a delightfully flirtatious manner, her chestnut hair catching the sunlight. "I grew up in these parts of the woods, mister. We don't like menfolk hereabouts called such names. Our men are good old boys."

He threw back his head and laughed at her husky voice until his ribs hurt.

"Did you really trade your car in," Ellie asked when his laugh mellowed to a chuckle, "or do you have both the car and Jeep now?"

"I traded it in. I'll probably be trading the Jeep soon."

"Why? Doesn't it run well?"

"When I showed Jess my new wheels, she said that fathers own vans."

It was like a curtain dropped over Ellie's face. It caused a shadow on his own good spirits.

Ellie busied herself with removing things from the wicker picnic hamper. "This is a lovely old basket."

"Anna said she and George took it on picnics. It hasn't been used since he died."

Ellie sat back on her heels and gazed at the basket. "That's rather bittersweet, isn't it? The basket must have brought back happy memories for her when she brought it out for us to use."

She continued unloading it: Red-and-white checked cloth napkins and colorful plastic plates and forks were followed by ham and cheese sandwiches on Anna's homemade sourdough buns, homemade watermelon pickles, potato chips that were definitely not homemade, and Anna's chocolate-cherry cake. "Nothing to drink?"

Travis retrieved sodas from the small cooler in the Jeep. When he returned, Ellie was holding a paperback copy of *In His Steps*. "I found this in the basket. Are you reading it?"

"Yes. I've known for awhile it's considered one of the classics of Christian literature, but I never made the time to read it before. When I discovered you were reading it, I decided to read it, too." He opened a can of soda and handed it to her. His gaze caught hers and held it. "I wanted to know what thoughts and stories fill your mind, what ideas you find fascinating."

She studied his eyes for what seemed a short lifetime. He didn't know what she was looking for. He allowed her to look her fill. He had nothing to hide.

He heard her swallow. "I think," she whispered, "that's the nicest thing you ever said to me."

Her words touched him deeply, making him feel strangely and unexpectedly humble. He hadn't known she would respond that way, hadn't known this would strike such a chord in her heart. He hadn't chosen to read the book to impress her.

He cleared his throat of an obstruction that seemed to have suddenly grown there. "It would be great if everyone lived by the motto in this book, wouldn't it—'What would Jesus do?' "

"Yes." Her smile was radiant. "Yes, it would."

Travis remembered Christmas Eve in the Los Angeles church when he'd prayed for Ellie to believe. Now they shared their belief. Peace enwrapped him. Whatever happened between himself and Ellie, at least their son was being raised by a wonderful woman who would teach Corey the joy of believing.

They were beginning their chocolate cake when Ellie came back to the subject of asking "What would Jesus do?" Her eyes looked troubled. "I love designing clothes and running the boutique, but sometimes I wonder whether Jesus would think it too materialistic a way for me to make a living."

Her statement would have shocked him in the days before she left Los Angeles. Now it seemed to him a natural thing for a person to wonder. "From where I stand, it looks like you are doing work for which He's gifted you, work that brings enjoyment to others. And in doing so, you give others an opportunity to earn a living and practice their own talents and skills. None of that sounds like a bad thing. I guess it boils down to your attitude."

"Mmmm. I guess." She gazed off at the peach tree-covered mountainside.

He allowed her to reflect in silence, or in nature's idea of silence. A light breeze stirred the redbud maples and fragrant pine trees. Small birds hopped about on the grass nearby, scratching in last autumn's crunchy leaves and chirping messages to one another. Were they hoping he and Ellie would leave some crumbs?

Ellie swallowed her last bite of cake. "There was a time you didn't think very highly of my designing." She studied her plate, scraping up the crumbs with her fork.

He chose his words carefully. He knew his attitude in the past had hurt her. "I wasn't too wise back then about a lot of things. I expect I still have a lot to learn, but some of the lessons are behind me. When I joined the Los Angeles firm, I thought in order to be successful we had to be carbon copies of the firm's other lawyers and their wives. I was wrong to want you to give up who you are. I'm sorry."

She studied his eyes as she had before, as though trying to probe into his soul. After a minute, she nodded. Moving to her knees, she started cleaning up their things and repacking the basket.

That's all? he thought. He tried to keep his frustration from showing. She'd acted like he'd given her the world's greatest jewel when he told her he wanted to know what ideas she found interesting, but when he admitted he'd been wrong about her life's work, she said nothing. He'd never understand women. But he wasn't going to quit trying to understand this one.

"Do you ever wonder about your own work, your law practice?" she asked.

"You mean, do I ever ask myself in my work, 'What would Jesus do?' "

She nodded.

"Sure. Maybe not in so many words, but yes."

"You don't find it compromising to practice law?"

"I try to practice Christ's love by serving my clients the best I can."

"Through legal actions?" Her voice was drenched with doubt.

"I help people whose legal rights are challenged. Don't you believe it's possible that can be a loving act?"

"Maybe, but there's so much conflict and pain in court battles. Doesn't the Bible tell us that we should go to court only as a last resort, that we should try to work things out first?"

"Yes, but there are legal acts that are necessary and don't hurt people, like making out wills, or examining documents to determine the legal status of a situation. What about people like Jess, who want to protect their children from violent fathers? You'd want her and Brent to have legal protection from Dan if it becomes necessary, wouldn't you?"

"Of course." Ellie shuddered visibly. "That reminds me. Chuck told me he saw Dan and Sissy together at a movie last Friday night."

Chills crawled up Travis's spine when she related her suspicion that Dan had left Brent home alone. Travis wouldn't be a bit surprised if Dan had done such a lowdown thing. "Did you ask Brent whether he had a babysitter?"

"I never think of it at the right time. If Dan did leave Brent alone, would a judge take his custody rights away?"

"Depends on the judge and the proof."

Ellie's shoulders slumped. "I guess a judge wouldn't take the word of a three-year-old boy."

"We could try to verify it, assuming he was left alone, that is."

"How?"

"First things first. We'll ask Brent if he had a babysitter last weekend."

"And if he says no?"

"We confront Dan."

"He'll lie."

"Most likely. So we'll ask him to give us the sitter's name and address."

"What if he refuses?"

"Then I'll threaten to talk to the local children's services."

"I'll ask Brent about the sitter when we get home. He might not remember, or might mix up that night with another time. I don't think he'd lie about it, but he is only three, and kids don't have a great sense of time at that age."

"We'll hope he remembers the name of a sitter and what a great time they had together."

"Yes. I worry and pray a lot about Jessica and Brent. I'm glad you're here to share this with."

Travis knew it was a huge admission for her to concede that she was leaning on him in any manner at all. "Then I'm glad I'm here, too."

Ellie took a deep breath and stood, lifting the blanket to shake it out. "There's a great waterfall near here. Want to see it before we head back?"

"Sure." Did he want to spend more time alone with her? Did birds fly? He felt like he was walking on air as they went back to the Jeep.

"Pull over here," Ellie said a few miles farther down the parkway.

Travis obediently pulled into the paved parking area of a well-marked lookout, one of many the parkway builders had provided so people could safely enjoy spectacular views of valleys and distant mountain ranges.

He looked out over the valley before them. It went on for miles and miles. "I don't see any waterfalls."

"You have to walk to the falls, silly. It will be good for you. Wear off that wonderful chocolate-cherry cake of Anna's." She pointed toward a wooded area to one side of the lookout parking lot. "The path to the waterfall is over there."

Travis climbed out of the Jeep after her. "Are you sure there's a path there? Maybe this isn't the right place." He saw nothing but trees and underbrush.

"The path's here." She headed toward the trees with a confident stride.

He followed, doubting.

Ellie tossed a triumphant look over her shoulder when they reached the trees. There was a path, two or three feet wide. She started down it.

Travis followed. Happiness for the simple time they were spending together bubbled up out of him. He hummed as they went along.

Ellie turned, stopping to stare at him with amusement written large across her face.

"What's so funny?"

"You're humming a Barney song."

Heat raced over his neck and face. Embarrassed laughter strangled his words. "How the mighty are fallen. A couple of months ago I was a big city lawyer attending symphonies and opening night movies and eating at spectacular restaurants among the rich and famous. Now I spend my evenings with a little boy whenever possible, watching Barney movies and dining at McDonald's—and loving it."

"I like this man better than the Los Angeles man."

Ellie's quiet words tied his heart and tongue into a tangle. She stood a few feet ahead of him, framed by rhododendron bushes and tall pines, watching him with her lips lifted in a small sweet smile. She'd never looked so attractive to him. He wanted to haul her into his arms and kiss her eyes, her neck, her lips—for starters.

Baby steps. He could barely hear the words through the roaring in his ears. Trying to break the spell, he did a little shuffle, his sneakers scuffing in the dirt path. "I do a pretty mean Barney dance, too."

Her laugh rang out. "I don't think directors will be breaking down your door to sign you to remake any Fred Astaire films." She pivoted and started off again. "We're getting closer to the falls. Can you hear them?"

He chuckled as he followed after her. And he'd thought the roaring he'd heard was his blood racing in his ears. Maybe some of it had been, but not all.

The path had been meandering down the hill. Now it steepened. He could see a wooden foot bridge with a peeled log railing crossing the river that came into view. Their footsteps quickened on the steep, twisting incline, and in a moment they were at the picturesque bridge.

They stopped in the middle, hands on the log that was worn smooth, and peered into the clear, shallow water gurgling beneath them over pebbles of golden, gray, and brown. The peaceful, cheerful sound fit his mood perfectly.

The gravel path continued on the other side of the bridge, continuing along the river. The waterfall's roar grew louder as they followed the path. Soon the path began a gradual descent, then a steeper descent, until the trail alternated between the gravel pathway and wooden stairs.

Eventually the trail led to a landing with a picturesque two-foot-high rock wall which offered limited protection to hikers. The falls were only beginning at this point. The water was shallow across the large flat stones.

Travis leaned over the wall to peer down the gorge. The river continued its sloping way toward the bottom. "Looks like it would make a great slide."

"Until you reached the drop-off a few hundred feet farther along."

Travis laughed at her dry tone.

She pointed to a wooden sign nearby. He read that people were to stay behind the rock wall, that the river's stones were slippery and people had fallen to their deaths on these falls. The news sobered him but took away none of his fascination with the river's beauty.

"There's another viewing point farther down the mountain." Ellie started off.

He reflected on the deceptive river as he and Ellie continued along the meandering path. It looked like a fun and beautiful place to play, but it was a deathtrap to those who didn't pay attention to nature's laws. *Like many places in life,* he thought, *when we don't listen to God's hints and continue on in situations where He has put up signs and rock walls telling us the places are unsafe. The situations look fun or beautiful, and we ignore the warnings to our peril.*

He shared his comparison with Ellie.

She smiled and nodded her agreement. "One of the things I love about living in the mountains are nature's lessons. God teaches us so many things about life through nature, if we'll only open our eyes and ears to learn the lessons."

Travis recalled her earlier comments about the storm opening up the forest's ceiling to sunlight for the forest's shorter plants. He noticed the rhododendrons along the path where man had opened an area of mountain forest to sunlight. He looked at the mighty tree trunks fallen in the nearby forest floor and the occasional trunk which had fallen across the path with new eyes.

When they reached the next viewing point, he exclaimed in delight. Above them the river ceased its lazy meandering down the mountain. It dropped in a thick white veil, spraying Travis and Ellie as it passed, and continuing to plummet toward the bottom of the mountain.

"This is certainly worth the climb." He couldn't see the bottom of the falls. He wondered how far they fell. "You were right about the drop."

A shiver ran through him. How frightening to be playing in the river and find yourself at the top of this huge drop with no chance of preventing yourself from falling along with the water.

"It's one of my favorite waterfalls." Ellie sat down on the rock ledge and watched the tumbling waters. "Jessica and I have brought Corey and Brent here a number of times."

"Do they like it?"

"They're fascinated by it. I don't think they understand what they're seeing yet."

Travis liked what he was seeing: Ellie seated in this natural setting with the magnificent waterfall for a background. He pulled a camera from the pocket of his lightweight tan jacket. He'd bought the camera to begin his own photo collection of

Corey. He wouldn't mind a few pictures of Corey's mother mingled in with those of Corey.

He caught her gazing at the falls. She turned her head immediately after he took the shot.

"Oh, no, not a picture." Her hands flew to her hair in an unnecessary attempt to straighten it.

"Your hair is fine. This will be a terrific shot. I'll make a copy for you if you'd like."

She wrinkled her nose. "No thanks. I see this face enough."

I wish I did, he thought, *like first thing every morning and last thing every night, for starters.* "It's a beautiful face."

Ellie flushed and changed the subject. "Why did you decide to move to Blackberry? I know you wanted to be part of Corey's life, but you could have done that without moving. You could have asked for shared custody."

"I didn't want to do that to my. . .our son." Travis sat down on the cold rocks beside her. "Taking him away from the only parent he knows for half the year," he shrugged, "what kind of love is that? He'd be terrified and lonely without you. He's too young to understand what shared custody means." Memories of other families with children of varying ages whose parents' divorces had been handled by his Los Angeles firm ran through his head. "Sometimes I think shared custody terrifies children of all ages."

"And their parents."

"Yes."

"You could have asked me to move back to Los Angeles with him."

"I had no right to ask you to move across the country for my convenience. You'd established a successful business here."

"There was a time when that would not have stopped you."

A hardness had crept into her tone. He chose his words cautiously. "There was a time when we had agreed to move together through life as one. Somewhere along the line, we started moving in different directions instead of taking the same path."

Sadness rolled across her face like a wave. She straightened her back and shoulders as though trying to throw off unhappy memories. "Moving to Blackberry was a major career decision. Don't you miss working for the Los Angeles firm? The famous clients, law cases that are unusual or involve lots of money, that are high profile, that take lots of research and new ways of interpreting the law?"

"I miss all of that. On the other hand, there's more variety in my everyday work here. I accepted a case last week that promises to be very interesting. A group of individuals concerned for the area's environmental integrity wants to limit a planned development."

"You must worry that, even if you return to Los Angeles eventually, you'll never be able to pick up where you left off in your career."

"I'd be lying if I said the thought hadn't occurred to me, and more than once or twice, but I know beyond doubt it was the right choice. More than anything else, I want to know Corey, to be there for him in every way I can."

Ellie stared at her hands in silence for a few moments, then stood.

"Ellie." Travis caught one of her hands and drew her gently toward him until she stood between his knees. He took her other hand also and played his thumbs along the smooth skin on the back of her hands.

He was surprised she'd allowed herself to be drawn so close to him, that she allowed him to hold her hands, that she allowed him this simple caress. He was almost afraid to speak for fear he would break the sweetness of the moment.

"What?"

Her breathless question forced him to speak. "I'd like to tell you about that night."

"What night?"

He knew by her defensive tone that she knew exactly what night he meant. "The night of the Christmas party in Los Angeles." The night that changed his life. Or had that night only been the culmination of a series of small choices he'd made in the days and months and years leading up to it, choices to put his own happiness above Ellie's, to put himself before his wife and before God?

Ellie took a step back. An emotionless shield seemed to drop over her eyes. He felt the pull of her hands, but she didn't tug them away. With immense gratitude for that tiny gift, he squeezed them tighter.

He waited for permission to speak before plunging into the place that had brought them both such pain. He wanted desperately for her to understand what had happened that night, but he wouldn't push her to open the wounded place in her heart so he could absolve himself.

He wondered if she could hear his heart beating over the rush of the waterfall behind them.

"All right."

Travis could hardly believe she'd agreed to his request. He realized he hadn't expected it. He'd imagined this discussion many times, but now he couldn't think how to start. He sent up a silent prayer asking God to give him the right words, that he might not cause Ellie to shut the door she'd just cracked open between them.

He stumbled into the beginning. "When I left our apartment that night I was furious. I drove around, telling myself all the reasons I was right to be angry and you were wrong to be angry." He shrugged and lifted one corner of his lips in an embarrassed grin. "The usual human reaction, I guess. Anyway, I found myself near Michelle's apartment and decided to stop. I thought she'd laugh at the idea that she and I were more than friends, and then I'd really be vindicated. Only she didn't laugh."

He continued with the story, telling Ellie what had happened in the apartment, how he happened to leave his cuff links behind, the whole sordid mess.

When he was done, he waited for her to say something. She didn't. The stiffness he'd felt in her at the beginning hadn't loosened an iota.

"Do you believe me, Ellie?"

"I don't know."

His heart sank. He'd begun with such hope. After all this time of refusing to listen, she'd allowed him to tell his story. She hadn't pulled away during the telling of it, and with each sentence he'd felt the excitement of hope rising within his chest. Now it fell and smashed, and he felt empty inside, not knowing what he could do to prove the truth of his story.

"I want to believe you."

Her unexpected admission sent the hope leaping up within him again. *Thank You, Lord.* "You do?"

"I want to, but I don't dare. Part of me is still terrified of trusting you."

Travis's throat thickened with tears he couldn't shed. "I'm sorry I hurt you."

"I know that you've made an incredible sacrifice moving to Blackberry to be near Corey. You've been wonderful with him. And I'm so grateful for the way you've helped Jessica out. I wish those things made the distrust go away. Maybe they should. I don't know. I only know, there's part of me that throws up flares and caution signs and says, 'Don't trust him. Don't let him in your heart again.' I don't dare not listen. Not yet. Maybe later."

Later wasn't as good as now, but it was a lot better than an outright rejection.

"Maybe never."

His heart plunged again. He stared at her hands, trying to accept what she was saying. Finally he nodded. "Thank you for listening anyway." He took a deep breath and looked up at her with a smile. "You're in charge of this expedition. We'll take it a day at a time. Baby steps."

"Baby steps."

The term brought a smile to her lips and the sparkle back to her eyes.

It loosened the tightness in his chest. If she could smile

with him like that, surely there was hope.

He stood quickly, dropping a quick kiss on her lips before she could step back. "To seal the bargain," he defended himself lightly. He gave her hands a squeeze before letting them go.

To his surprise she didn't move. A wistful longing looked out from her brown eyes. Her lips, which had been so warm and soft beneath his brief touch, were open slightly.

"I wish I could trust you," she whispered. "Sometimes, I miss you. I miss us."

"I do, too." His heart hammered. Where was she taking them?

Ellie lifted both hands and laid them against his cheeks. He barely breathed, drinking in the wonder of her soft caress. Rising on her tiptoes, she touched her lips to his, gently, in a kiss that lingered longer than his quick peck. He returned it, slowly, not forcing it into something more passionate.

Ellie groaned softly against his lips and leaned against him, her arms slipping around his neck.

Travis's arms held her close. He buried his face in her neck, loving the feel of her skin, the familiar scent of her light floral cologne, the silkiness of her hair against his cheek.

She gasped slightly as he kissed her on the side of her neck, the place that he'd always delighted in knowing she loved to be kissed. He held her tighter, rejoicing that she was in his arms again, that she was there of her own choice.

He wasn't sure how many minutes passed before she withdrew slowly from his arms. Too few minutes to satisfy him, more than he knew he'd had a right to hope for.

With a shaky smile, Ellie turned to start up the path. Travis took her hand, and she allowed him to hold it. He watched her from the corner of his eye whenever he dared take his gaze from the path, loving the slightly mussed hair and flushed cheeks that were a visible reminder of the intimate minutes they'd spent.

Maybe never.

The words whispered through his thoughts, reminding him that kisses aren't guarantees.

eleven

Ellie's thoughts tumbled through her mind and her emotions through her body as the water tumbled over the rocks in the river they left behind as they climbed up to Travis's Jeep. Her cheeks were still warm from the time she and Travis had spent in each others' arms.

She kept her gaze out the windows while they drove back to Blackberry, not willing to look into his face and possibly see his desire for her there.

Had she been a fool, kissing him that way? Undoubtedly. But it felt so good.

In the years between her departure from Los Angeles and Travis's arrival in Blackberry, she'd kept the door slammed and locked on their intimate memories. Once she'd let him through that door when he'd kissed her in her hallway weeks earlier, she'd been allowing herself to remember the early days of their romance and marriage, how special and beautiful his kisses and touch had been to her.

You'll be sorry for those kisses later, she admonished herself.

Her emotions weren't ready to go along with logic and reality. They were still wrapped up in Travis's kisses.

Ellie was out of the Jeep almost before it stopped in her drive-way. "Thanks for a wonderful afternoon."

"Wait, Ellie."

She waved over her shoulder, grinning a broad friendly grin, and pretending she hadn't heard his plea.

She could as well have waited. He was beside her with a few long strides. "Mind if I say hello to Corey?"

Ellie's ego deflated instantly. "Of course."

Their kisses so occupied her mind that she'd forgotten he would want to see their son.

132

She groaned silently. Had she created a hopeless emotional pool of quicksand when she kissed Travis? For Corey's sake if not her own she mustn't allow her physical attraction to Travis to muddle her decisions.

At the front door she laid a hand on Travis's chest. "Wait. There's something I must say."

He waited while she struggled for the right words.

She took a deep breath, then blurted, "About the kiss—"

"Kisses." His smile teased her.

"Yes, well, about them." She linked her fingers, twisting them back and forth while she fumbled. "I don't want you to think I meant. . .that I didn't mean. . ."

"I know." He cupped the side of her neck with one hand and lifted her chin with a thumb. "Your kisses didn't mean you trust me."

She nodded, part of her glad he understood, part of her miserable.

"I hope," he continued, "they meant you're trying to forgive me and believe in me again."

"Yes." That was exactly what they'd meant, though she hadn't understood it herself until he put it into words.

"You're in charge. If I start moving too fast, say so and I'll slow down. I promise." His hand at her neck drew her only close enough for him to drop a kiss on her forehead. "Let's go see our son."

The house was very still when they entered. Ellie called out, but no one answered. "They're probably in the back yard."

But they weren't.

"That's strange." Uneasiness spread tentacles in Ellie's chest.

"It's five o'clock. Maybe Jess took the boys out to eat."

"Probably. Or to Anna's."

"Or to the park. They love the playground there."

Ellie reminded herself there was no reason for her to experience the uneasiness that wasn't quite fear. The tentacles only grew and gripped harder.

"Maybe Jess left a note," Travis suggested.

Ellie ran back inside, allowing the screen door to slam behind her, and hurried to the kitchen table, willing a note to be there.

There wasn't one.

"This is where we leave notes for each other," she told Travis when he reached her. "There's nothing here."

His arms went around her shoulders from behind. He gave her a comforting squeeze. "Don't make up any awful scenarios in your mind. Maybe Jess took the boys on a picnic. Remember how they were clamoring to join us on ours?"

"Jessica and I share a car. It's parked in the drive."

"So maybe they went for a walk."

"You're right. I'm being silly. Any minute they'll walk in the door and I'll feel like a fool for worrying."

She didn't even dare voice her fear that one of the boys had been hurt and Jessica had taken him to the clinic or to the hospital in a neighboring town. Travis would think she was hysterical. Besides, Jessica would have left a note in such a case.

"Maybe they're in the garage. Jessica uses it for her studio." Ellie hurried toward the back door. "Jessica usually doesn't allow the boys in there. She thinks it's too dangerous with her tools and paints and all."

Jessica and the boys weren't in the studio either.

"They're fine," Travis insisted. "You're going to make yourself sick worrying this way. Why don't you come back to Anna's with me? Visiting with her will keep your mind off fictional problems. You can leave a note asking Jess to call when she gets back."

It was the sensible thing to do, of course. Yet when they were back in the Jeep, Ellie asked Travis to drive past the park and check the store before going to Anna's. Ellie was glad when Travis did as she asked without ridiculing her fears further, but they didn't see Jessica and the boys.

They weren't at Anna's either, nor had Anna heard from them since church that morning.

Ellie consciously pushed away her fears. She complimented Anna on the picnic lunch and listened to Anna's stories about her own and George's experiences with the picnic hamper. Travis and Ellie told Anna of their afternoon—leaving out the kisses.

Through it all, Ellie never stopped straining to hear the phone's ring announcing the call from Jessica. The call never came.

In the middle of one of Anna's stories about her and George's experiences as young parents when their first child was Corey's age, a picture flashed in Ellie's mind: an ornate, oval, brass doorhandle plate.

Ellie went cold from head to foot. She turned to Travis. "The doors weren't locked."

His eyebrows scrunched together. "What?"

"The doors at my house. They weren't locked. We always lock them now when we go out, because of Dan's threats."

She saw by the way his eyes widened slightly that he realized the implications, but his voice and manner were reassuring.

"There weren't any signs of struggle in the house. How about in Jess's studio?"

"No, everything looked normal there, too."

"Then most likely Jess forgot to lock the doors." Travis grinned. "A person can forget anything while trying to keep up with Corey and Brent."

That was true. Ellie's alarm calmed somewhat but didn't go away. Anna picked up her story and Ellie pretended to turn her attention back to it.

Before long Travis stood and stretched. "Think I'll run down to the grocery store and pick up some soda. I'm about out."

The waiting was harder after he left. At least he wouldn't be gone long, Ellie thought, turning her attention to a new lace design Anna was showing her.

❧

Travis stood inside Sheriff Strand's door and finished telling the little bit there was to tell about Jessica and the boys. "I know there isn't any reason to believe there's been any. . .foul play, but I thought. . .just in case something's wrong here, I wanted you to know."

The sheriff's round face looked grim. "I'm glad you came to me. There's no big city police department here, just me. I know almost everyone in this town. I don't have to be told Ellie knows Jessica's habits. If Ellie says it's unusual for Jessica to take the boys somewhere without leaving a note, then it's unusual. I don't like it that the house is unlocked, not with what I've seen of Dan's temper over the years."

"His house was dark when I drove past, but I didn't stop to see if he was there."

"I'll check it out. But first I'll try Doc Swenson and then the nearest hospital."

Travis paced the small entryway while Sheriff Strand made his calls. *Corey's fine. They're all fine. There's nothing to worry about. This is only a precaution.* He repeated the phrases again and again. They did nothing to stop the fear that rose like bile in his stomach.

"Doc hasn't seen them, and there's no record of any of them checking in at the hospital." The sheriff grabbed his official brown leather jacket from the closet.

"If you're heading to Dan's, I want to come along."

Strand hesitated with his hand on the doorknob. "I should order you home, but I won't. Follow in your own vehicle if you want. See that you stay in it. I don't want any fool John Wayne-type stunts. If Dan's home, I'll talk to him alone. Got it?"

"Got it."

Travis was glad to be doing something, even something as mundane as following Strand to Dan's house. Sitting around waiting for Jess and the boys was making him crazy. He knew Ellie felt the same. Part of him wanted to be with her, comforting and reassuring her, but if there was any chance Jess and the boys needed help getting back home, he wanted to make sure they had every possibility of receiving that help.

He hadn't anticipated how difficult it would be to stay in the car once they were at Dan's. He watched as Sheriff Strand knocked at the front door of the darkened house, then watched him walk around to the back. Travis gripped the wheel so tight his hands hurt.

The sheriff peered into windows as he made his way back to the cars. Travis realized he could barely make out the man's form. The sun was setting. Travis had never minded that the mountains made the sun appear to set earlier than in flat lands. Now the evening darkness was like an enemy.

Sheriff Strand stopped beside Travis's window. "Nothing there. Can't go inside without a warrant, as you know, and I don't have a legitimate reason to request one yet. Dan's Mercedes is in the garage, but his new pickup is gone. Let's drive by his office."

Dan wasn't at his office.

Travis remembered Dan's girlfriend, Sissy, and mentioned her to the sheriff.

"I know where she lives."

Sissy was home, but she hadn't seen Dan.

They headed back to Ellie's, hoping Jessica had turned up and that the men were on a wild goose chase.

The house was as still as Travis and Ellie had left it hours before.

Travis flipped on lights and checked the kitchen table. No note.

The sheriff hiked at his pants. "Did Ellie check to see if anything was missing? Kid's clothes, toys, Jess's clothes, a suitcase, that sort of thing?"

"No. You don't think Jess kidnaped the kids, do you?"

"One thing I've learned in law enforcement. Usually it's people the victims know who hurt them, the very people they're most apt to trust."

Travis's stomach turned over at the word *victims*. It brought his worst fears too close to home. He knew from his law practice that what Sheriff Strand said about victims knowing the people who harm them was true. "So now, assuming something is amiss here, we have at least two suspects, Dan and Jess."

"Why don't you get Ellie back here to check on what's missing? Before you leave, do you know where Ellie keeps pictures? A clear picture of Jessica and the boys might be a good thing to have to show around. While you're picking up Ellie, I'll start asking neighbors if they saw anything suspicious around here this afternoon."

Travis could have kicked himself for not thinking of speaking to the neighbors earlier, but he'd believed at first that Ellie was making a mountain out of a mole hill, being a typical worry-wart mom.

Travis didn't have to dig out the albums. Pictures of Ellie and Jess and the boys were displayed all over the house. He selected one with Jess and the boys kneeling in front of the Christmas tree, grins on all their faces, Jess's arms about the boys. It was a good likeness of each of them.

When he arrived at Anna's, Ellie's first words were, "That was a long trip for soda pop." She looked pointedly at his empty arms. "Didn't the station have any?"

Travis had forgotten there weren't any stores open on Sundays in Blackberry, only the super station on the edge of town. Ellie must have suspected all along he'd left about the boys.

He sat down on the sofa near Ellie's chair, not bothering to remove his coat. In a few sentences and in as emotionless a tone as he could manage he told Ellie and Anna what he'd been doing. "Sheriff Strand wants you to go home and check to see if anything's missing."

Ellie's face went white.

Travis thought she might scream or faint or react like women in movies and books so often do when faced with a frightening situation. Then he realized she'd been facing for hours the possibility that the boys were in danger. He was the one who hadn't believed it right away.

She stood. "All right. Let's go."

Anna stood, too, laying a wrinkled hand on Ellie's arm. "I'll go with you." She hurried to the hall closet to retrieve her and Ellie's coats.

Travis put his arms around Ellie. Her arms gripped his waist like a vise, but only for a moment. Then she pulled away, her face set as if in stone.

His heart ached for her pain, and for his own.

Corey's fine, he assured himself for the umpteenth time. *All this is just precautionary.*

By the time they reached Ellie's place, sleet started falling, nasty little pellets that drove the doubts in Travis's mind into full-fledged fears that twisted his gut. He'd forgotten the snowstorm that was predicted to move in.

The sheriff wasn't at the house. Ellie made a quick pass through the downstairs. "Nothing missing down here but the spring jackets Jess and the boys would have worn."

They were coming down from her upstairs search when Sheriff Strand returned.

"Anything missing?"

Ellie described the outfits she thought the three were wearing.

"Sure about that?" Sheriff Strand had a pencil poised over a small notebook.

"I'm sure about the boys' outfits. I'm pretty sure about Jessica's."

Strand's pencil scratched across the pad. "Anything else missing?"

"The gray stuffed pony Travis gave Corey. That's not unusual. Corey carries it everywhere."

Travis's heart expanded. If Corey was in trouble, Travis hoped the pony made him feel braver, safer, loved.

The smell of fresh coffee wafted into the hallway and brought a small smile to Travis's lips. Anna was already at work in the kitchen.

There was a knock at the door and Ellie opened it. "Mike.

What are you doing here?"

"Sheriff asked me to stop over."

Travis recognized the man but had never met him. He ran a local shop that performed a number of services businesses and individuals in a small town needed. He provided one location for people to copy things, fax things, use a computer, make posters, and use various shipping services.

Mike gave the sheriff a friendly smile. "What do you need?"

Sheriff Strand handed him the picture of Jess and the boys.

Ellie gasped in recognition, one hand flying to cover her mouth.

Travis slipped an arm around her shoulders.

Strand darted them a glance before answering Mike. "Can you make up some copies of these, quick like? Maybe some blowups, too."

Mike shrugged. "Sure. What's the problem?"

"Not sure there is any yet," Strand answered. "Just taking some precautions." He explained the situation succinctly.

"I'll get them back here as soon as I can." Mike sent a pitying glance over Strand's broad shoulder to Ellie. "Sorry, Ellie. Hope this is just a false alarm."

Sheriff Strand spoke over his shoulder as he walked out with Mike. "I'm going to make some calls from my car. I want your line kept clear, Ellie, in case Jessica tries to call you."

The sleet had turned to snow, and the dusk to dark. Travis could hear the *shhh-ing* of the snow flakes, could see them thick in the light from the old-fashioned street lamp before he closed the door behind the two men. Usually he loved the beauty and winter-wonderland sense such a snow brought. Tonight it chilled his bones.

Travis wondered whether the sheriff was putting out a bulletin on Jessica and the boys. It was early in the game for that, but Travis hoped the lawman was doing it anyway.

When the sheriff returned, he and Travis and Ellie moved into the living room.

Travis sat beside Ellie on the sofa and reached for her hand. "Did you have any success with the neighbors, Sheriff?"

"No one saw anything or anyone unusual."

"Dan?"

"No one saw him, either."

Travis's shoulders dropped. He hadn't realized how much he'd hoped one of the neighbors had seen something that would explain everything or that Jessica had told one of them where she and the kids were going.

Strand lowered himself to the edge of an overstuffed, worn maroon chair. "I have some questions for you two. Travis gave me a rundown on the situation, but I want to hear everything again from the beginning, from both of you."

The questions were simple and straightforward. When had they last seen Jessica and the boys, where exactly had Travis and Ellie spent the afternoon, had anyone else been with them, when had they noticed Jessica and the boys missing, was there a vehicle Jessica might be driving?

Travis and Ellie answered everything honestly. Travis knew Sheriff Strand needed the information. Travis had no qualms in answering the questions fully and completely and knew Ellie felt the same. Yet memories of newscasts with other parents of missing children flashed before him, parents who begged convincingly for their children's safe return, only to be exposed later as their children's killers. And he knew that in Sheriff Strand's mind, he and Ellie had been added to the list of suspects.

It was a strange feeling, but as a lawyer Travis knew the sheriff was acting wisely in considering them suspects. Secure in their innocence, the knowledge wasn't disturbing.

The questioning was interrupted by the arrival of two deputies. While Sheriff Strand was talking with them in the hall, Anna brought in a tray with mugs of coffee, cream, sugar, and doughnuts.

Anna set the tray on the coffee table. "I found these doughnuts in the cookie jar."

"Thanks, but I'm not hungry right now." Ellie gave Anna a slight smile.

"Maybe not, but have a doughnut anyway. They're calming."

Travis wondered whether that was true. If it were, wouldn't the caffeine in the coffee counteract the doughnuts?

Anna must have anticipated the question. "Decaffeinated. I made a pot of each." She winked at them. "I'd like Sheriff Strand to stay awake until Jessica and the boys arrive home."

Travis couldn't help grinning at her attempt to lighten their emotions for a moment. Tension made the air in the room feel thicker than the snow flake-filled air outside.

Anna sat down beside Ellie on the edge of the sofa cushion and patted Ellie's hand. "I made a quick call to Pastor Evanson. He and his wife will make calls to start a prayer chain. I didn't want to make any more calls. I thought you'd want to keep the line clear."

Ellie clutched Anna's hand with both her own. "Thank you."

"Thanks." Travis's voice was husky. He'd learned to rely on his own prayers and those of friends in the last year or so, but never had the prayers meant so much. Travis believed in the power of prayer, but before tonight he hadn't understood what an expression of love it was to pray for another.

As the evening wore on concerns for the safety of the missing people increased. The storm grew in intensity. Wind picked up, driving the snow into a whirling, biting enemy. The wind whistled around the corners of the house, rattling the storm windows and making it impossible to forget the storm's ferocity.

Ellie stared out the front window, hugging her arms over the sweatshirt she was still wearing. "They were only wearing spring jackets. I hope they are someplace warm."

Travis slipped his arms around her from the back and drew her against his chest, resting his cheek on her hair, wishing he could absorb all her fear and pain into himself.

Beside them, Sheriff Strand said, "Wherever they are,

they're likely holed up. From the Highway Patrol's reports, it sounds as if the roads will soon be impassable if they aren't already."

Travis felt a shiver run through Ellie and hugged her tighter, knowing that like him she was imagining Corey freezing in the winter storm. "Jess is with the boys," he reminded her. "She'd lay down her life to protect them, you know that. She'll take care of them."

Ellie nodded and patted his hand.

He hoped she wasn't thinking what he was thinking: that there were limits to Jess's ability to protect the boys. He believed what he'd said, that she'd give her life for the boys. He only hoped Jess didn't have to do just that.

❧

As evening grew into night, people began stopping by. Neighbors came with sympathy and food. Pastor Evanson came to pray with Ellie and Travis and stayed on to support them. He reassured them that all the members of their church family his wife had called had readily agreed to partake in the prayer chain.

Mike returned with the enlarged copies of the Christmas picture and a sample of a poster with the three faces smiling large at the viewers.

"Great," Sheriff Strand approved. "Make up some more of these posters. Charge them to my office."

"I'll get right on them." Mike yanked on his gloves. "There'll be no charge."

Travis gripped his hand. "Thanks." He could barely get the word past the lump in his throat.

Mike gave a sharp nod, then hugged Ellie. "Keep your chin up, kid." A minute later he headed back into the storm.

"I'm going back to the office." Sheriff Strand was pulling on his jacket. "I want to get these pictures distributed and put the news out over the wire. Other law enforcement agencies or other emergency groups trying to reach us will try my office first."

Travis knew it was the wisest move, but he wished the sheriff wasn't leaving. It made Travis feel left out of the information loop.

"Deputy Rogers will stay here." The sheriff nodded toward a tall young man with curly red hair cut so short it looked crispy. "He'll have a short-wave radio and a hand-held radio to keep in touch with my office in case the phone lines go down."

Travis's stomach tightened. He hadn't even thought of that possibility.

"I'd better get candles and flashlights together, just in case." Ellie started toward the dining room.

Anna followed. "We'd best make extra coffee, too. Mrs. Schneider from next door brought over an urn. The coffee will stay warm quite awhile in there."

Travis wandered into the dining room after Ellie. The old print of the cabin beneath tall pines on a snow-covered mountain caught his attention. He remembered telling Jessica he thought it looked like a romantic spot, a place of rustic beauty and serenity. Now it only spoke to him of a cold, dangerous land.

Ellie was looking through drawers, pulling out candles of various sizes and colors. Travis wished he had something to do, anything at all to take his mind off Corey. Something besides praying, that was. The same prayer had been running through his mind for hours, *Keep them safe, Lord. Please, keep them safe.*

It was almost midnight when Travis heard footsteps crossing the porch in running thumps. Even with the snow cover and all the people coming and going, these were distinctive in their rush and the loudness that spoke of the person's urgency. The door crashed open before Travis could reach it.

twelve

Ellie heard the door crash, followed by Travis's shocked, "Dan!"

She ran through the living room to the front door. "Dan, what are you doing here? I thought. . ." She snapped back the incriminating words on the tip of her tongue, the belief that he was with Jessica and the boys, that he was responsible for their disappearance.

The wind howled through the door, whisking in snow. Travis shut it out.

Dan wasn't wearing his usual long khaki coat. Instead he was dressed in jeans, a flannel shirt, and a lightweight jacket, all of which were covered in snow. His hiking boots dripped melting snow onto the hallway runner. His eyes were wide, and his chest lifted and fell with his panting. "Have you heard anything about the boys yet?"

Ellie shook her head. "Not yet."

Travis stepped beside her, arms crossed over his chest. "How did you hear about them, Dan? Stopped by your place to tell you about them, but you weren't there. Figured you were out of town."

"I was. Tax season just ended. Needed a break. I got back in town about ten minutes ago. Barely got out of my truck before one of my neighbors rushed over and told me the boys and Jessie are missing."

Deputy Rogers stood behind Dan. He'd moved so quietly that Ellie hadn't heard him coming. "When was the last time you saw them, Dan?"

"Me?" Dan shrugged. "This afternoon."

"When? Where?" Rogers' questions were asked in a friendly, eager tone. "We need all the information we can get."

Ellie wondered whether the officer trusted Dan as much as he appeared to.

"I stopped over early, not long after noon. Jessie said Ellie had just left with Travis for a picnic in the mountains. So I invited Jessie and the boys to drive over to Blowing Rock for lunch."

"Why Blowing Rock?"

"The boys like the fast-food restaurants, and we don't have any of the chain restaurants here."

"That's true, the boys love those places," Ellie confirmed.

"What did you do after lunch?" The officer was writing Dan's information down in his trusty notebook.

"Came back here and dropped them off. Then I took off for a drive in the mountains. Nowhere special. I just wanted to get away. Like I said, tax season is finally over. Haven't had too many minutes to call my own the last few months."

What minutes he'd had, he'd spent with Sissy rather than his son, Ellie thought.

She wandered away, not wanting to be near Dan. He made her skin crawl, treating Jessica and Brent the way he did and then acting the concerned husband and father.

Her conscience nipped. Even though he wasn't the epitome of the perfect father, she shouldn't assume he didn't care whether Brent was safe.

Back in the dining room, she opened the door of the built-in china cabinet and reached for a pair of pottery candlesticks. She gasped when large hands settled on her shoulders. Relaxed when she realized they belonged to Travis. He kneaded her shoulder and neck muscles. "Mmmm. That feels good."

"Your muscles are so tied up in knots you could qualify for a human pretzel."

She let him work at the knots.

"What do you think about Dan's alibi?" he asked.

Alibi? she wondered. "It's not like Jessica to go to lunch with Dan, with or without the boys."

"That's what I thought, but I expect he's too smart to lie about it. He must know all our stories will be checked out."

"They'll have a hard time verifying ours." She laid her hands over his, which were still on her shoulders. "I'm so afraid. I was sure Jessica and the boys were with Dan. There was no proof, but I was so sure. Now. . .they could be anywhere, with anyone."

"Wherever they are, God is there, too."

She wished that comforted her more. She supposed it should make the fear go away, but awful things happened to lots of people even though God was there with them. What would she do if something awful happened to Corey? How would she go on?

Anger at her lack of control of the situation rose inside her until she wanted to scream and scream and scream. She knew that wouldn't help. The anger kept churning inside her instead.

"It looks like Dan's decided to stay." Travis nodded toward the living room.

Dan, minus his jacket and wet hiking boots, was pacing the floor, rubbing his hands together, looking for all the world like a worried, loving father.

Deputy Rogers came back into the dining room with a hot mug of coffee and a sugar cookie, which Ellie recognized as a contribution from one of the neighbors.

"Shouldn't someone let Eric. . .I mean, Sheriff Strand, know Dan's here?" Ellie asked.

"I called him." Rogers spoke around a bite of cookie. "He'll probably stop by after awhile to talk to Dan."

The dining-room table looked like a command post with the deputy's radio, notebooks, and maps. Rogers opened one of the maps and studied it, leaning over the table to do so.

Ellie wondered whether he was looking for anything special or just trying to keep from being bored while they waited. She wished she could think of something to do to keep her mind off Corey and all sorts of horrible possibilities. *Keep him safe, Lord. Keep them all safe.* The refrain never stopped running through her mind.

It was past midnight. Neighbors' visits had dribbled off and finally stopped. Pastor Evanson was still there, sometimes talking quietly with one person or another, sometimes sitting by himself and, Ellie was sure, praying. Faithful Anna was still there, too, offering coffee and food to people without pushing it on them, offering comforting pats and hugs, neither giving false hope nor voicing despair.

The night went on forever.

Or so it seemed to Ellie. Logic told her dawn would come eventually. Honesty told her dawn would banish darkness but not the fear that was burning inside her.

She tried to avoid looking at the pictures of the boys and at their toys strewn around the house. She was afraid she'd break down and start crying if she paid those things too much mind, and if she let herself start crying, she might never be able to stop.

When dawn came, there was no blush on the horizon. The only announcement of its arrival was a lightening of the outside world. The storm still swirled around the house and through the village streets and valley and over the surrounding mountains. The winds still howled and the snow still fell.

"We must have had eighteen inches of snow so far." Dan blew on his clasped hands as though he were outside in the fierce cold.

Beside him, Ellie stared at his hands. "What happened to your thumb?" It was purple beneath the nail.

Surprise registered on his face. He looked at his hand as if it was a foreign object, then stuffed it into his back pocket. "Slammed it in my truck door."

Ellie winced. "Nothing more painful than that."

"That's for sure."

Ellie looked out the window at the white blanket covering the ground, walks, and street.

Dan shook his head. "No one's going to be able to get

through that to help the kids and Jessie."

"Don't say that." Ellie clenched her fists. She was so angry at him she could spit, but all he'd done was say aloud what she'd been thinking, what she didn't want to believe.

Travis looked like he'd like to slug Dan. "Ellie's right. We must keep believing Jess and the boys are okay, that we'll find a way to find them, or they'll find their way back to us."

"There are ways to get around out there." Rogers appeared with his ever-present coffee mug. "Snowmobiles, snowshoes, skis, four-wheel drives. Sheriff contacted me a few minutes ago. He's been making some calls, arranging search parties."

Hope shot through Ellie, dashing away her fatigue. She grabbed the deputy's arm. "Are they really planning to go out in this storm? I hadn't dared hope—"

"They'll head out as soon as the winds die down enough that we don't have to worry about losing anyone else on the mountains."

Ellie's spirits were dampened but not drowned. Surely the winds would calm before too long. The storm had already been raging for more than twelve hours. *You control the winds, Lord. You calmed the sea in the Bible. You can calm the wind now. Please. Please.*

There wasn't any question in anyone's mind that something was terribly wrong. Everyone knew Jessica would have found a way to get news to Ellie about her and the boys' whereabouts if at all possible. Jessica would never have let Ellie worry overnight and through a major storm.

Unless she wants to disappear with the kids herself. Ellie tried to push away the thought, but it persisted. Finally she broached the possibility to Travis in a corner of the living room where they couldn't be overheard.

Travis shook his head. "Why would Jess do that?"

"To get Brent away from Dan."

"She wouldn't be so cruel as to take Corey, too, keeping his location a secret from you. If the plan had been to keep Brent from Dan, Jess would have left Corey with Anna or Pastor

Evanson or one of the neighbors."

Ellie sighed and pushed her hair back off her forehead. "You're right. I hate that I would even entertain the possibility that Jessica would steal the boys away."

"You can be sure that Sheriff Strand has considered the possibility."

The whine of a snowmobile screamed up the street and stopped in front of the house. Ellie darted a curious glance at Travis and moved to the window. She couldn't make out who the rider was who made his way through knee-high snow to the front porch. The person was wearing a helmet and dressed head to toe in a thick black and purple snowmobile suit.

Once inside with his helmet off, Ellie was touched to see it was Chuck who had made his way through the early morning storm. He pulled off his thick gloves and touched her face with a cold hand. "You doing okay?"

"I'm holding up." She pressed his hand with her own warm one for a moment in an expression of thanks.

"I had to come over and check for myself before heading to the sheriff's office."

"You're going out to look for Corey?"

"Yes."

Gratitude filled her like a physical thing. Tears smarted her eyes. She beat them back. "Are they planning to start out soon?"

He hesitated slightly. "As soon as possible."

She knew he meant when the winds died down, as Deputy Rogers had said.

"I'd like to be in the search party."

Ellie whirled around at Travis's announcement. He hadn't made it to her but to Rogers.

Rogers shrugged. "No one can keep you from joining it if you want."

"Me, too."

Dan's declaration surprised Ellie even more than Travis's.

Rogers raised his red eyebrows. "You both understand the

party will work in teams or groups. We don't want to lose anyone out there."

Both men nodded.

"Neither of you needs to do this," Rogers assured. "We have plenty of volunteers, experienced and otherwise. The ski rescue team from the resort will be helping out. Sheriff's even arranged for a helicopter once the weather allows."

Neither man backed out.

"I'd better head home and change," Travis said.

"I have an extra snowmobile suit if you need one," Chuck offered.

"Thanks, but I think my ski outfit will do. Can I talk to you for a minute?" Travis held out a hand to Ellie.

Curious, she took it and walked with him to the dining room where they could speak privately.

He placed his hands on her shoulders and looked into her eyes. "I won't go if you want me to stay."

"Thank you." Her tight throat made the words a whisper. "I appreciate your offer, but I'll be all right. Anna is still here, though she's finally napping, and Pastor Evanson and Deputy Rogers. Now that morning's here, I'm sure friends will be stopping again. Do what you feel you must."

"You're sure?"

"Yes. I understand that you want to be out there looking for Corey. Part of me wants to do that, too. But I want to be here for Corey if. . .when he comes home. Maybe you should get some sleep before you go out, though." Reddish-gray circles beneath blue eyes showed he hadn't slept all night.

"I couldn't sleep now." He pulled her into his embrace with his arms around her shoulders. His stubble caught at her hair, but she didn't mind. "I'm praying for Corey and the others all the time," he said. "I'll be praying for you, too."

She smiled a bittersweet smile into his shoulder before lifting her chin enough to say, "I'll be praying for you, too. Be careful out there."

Ellie darted a quick glance at herself in the mirror over the dining room bureau. She had circles beneath her eyes as deep and dark as Travis's. Her hair was a dirty mess. With a start she remembered she hadn't brushed it since she and Travis had shared kisses on the mountain trail beside the waterfall.

She ran a hand over her hair when they started back to join the others, then shrugged. It was only hair. What did it matter what it looked like at a time like this?

"I'll have to call Mom and Dad." She dreaded it. "The news will all but kill them, but they need to know."

Travis agreed. "It would be worse if the news services got hold of the story and your folks heard about Corey first in a newscast."

"Dan's left already," Chuck informed them. "If you want, I'll run you over to your place on my snowmobile, Travis."

The men left minutes later. Ellie stood alone at the window, watching the whining machine carry them away into the snow. She shivered.

thirteen

Eight hours later Travis shivered as he slid off another snow-mobile in front of the sheriff's office. He'd never been so cold in his life, in spite of all the time he'd spent skiing in the Rockies. It wasn't that he wasn't dressed for the weather. The sheriff had handed out hand warmers in the form of dry heat. They looked like small bandages. Travis had them stuffed into his mittens and boots. They'd helped, but they couldn't keep the cold out forever.

Maybe because the chill he felt wasn't all from the weather.

Every minute his fears for Corey, Brent, and Jess grew. The fears were like a rain forest out of control, smothering the life from his heart.

Ellie must feel the same. I should be with her, he thought.

The man walking beside him slapped him on the back. "Maybe we'll have some good news inside."

Travis forced a smile through cracked lips. "Maybe."

Sheriff Strand hadn't good news. He shook his head and sighed, staring at the floor, before lifting bloodshot eyes to meet Travis's gaze. "It's dark. We've had to call in all the searchers. We can't have people running around in the mountains at night."

Travis nodded, numbness enveloping him. His mind understood the logic, but his heart cried out against it.

"We're fortunate the wind died down this morning and let us get out today at all."

Travis nodded again. He looked around the room. It was filled with searchers who were watching him with pity in their eyes or avoiding his gaze so he wouldn't see their pity. He recognized many of the men and women, but not all. Some attended the church. Some ran local businesses. Some worked in local shops. The owner of the Black Bear restaurant was there, and so was the waitress who served him coffee and pancakes every morning. The owner of the local dry cleaners where Travis had his suits cleaned was there. The editor of the small Blackberry newspaper was there—to help, not to get a story. Then there was the mechanic from the shop where he'd had the Jeep serviced, the man who ran the garbage truck, the woman who ran the small local greenhouse and serviced the plants at his office, the photographer whose work hung in the hallway at the law office, and one of the church deacons. And Chuck.

Travis tried to swallow the lump in his throat. He'd never felt so much love directed toward him in his entire life. "Thanks. Thanks to all of you for coming out. You can't know how much this means to Ellie and me."

They started filing out, heading for home. Each one shook his hand or laid a hand on his arm or said a word of sympathy or encouragement as they passed. Almost all of them said they'd be back at dawn.

"I know when people are missing in Los Angeles there's a lot of angels on earth out looking for them," Travis told Sheriff Strand, "but mostly those human angels are people who search for missing people as part of their job. These people. . ." He was at a loss for words.

"Every one of them knows it could be them or someone they love lost on a mountain next time."

"We don't even know Jess and the boys are out there. They could be anywhere. They could have caught a plane in Charlotte and be in the West Indies, for all we know."

"Yep, but we don't believe that, do we?"

Travis studied the sheriff's face, not certain what the law officer thought. "No, at least I don't. I think they're out in these mountains, but I don't have a tangible reason for believing that."

"There's still people out searching, but I've called all the teams in. Dan's with one of them. They should be here shortly." Strand's shoulders heaved. "Sorry we haven't discovered any sign of your son."

He's taking it as if it's a personal defeat, Travis thought. "Something keeps tugging at my mind, as though the Lord's trying to remind me of something, but it's just out of reach."

"I know the feeling. Frustrating."

"It sure is."

❧

After a hot shower and change of clothes at Anna's, Travis headed back to Ellie's house. His mind felt as fuzzy as an open pussy willow. The lack of sleep combined with the emotional turbulence inside him was taking its toll.

A snowplow had been out during the day, and his Jeep made the short journey to Ellie's house easily, though the roads were anything but clear by Los Angeles standards.

Ellie's house was lit from top to bottom. A number of vehicles lined the street and filled her driveway. Someone had shoveled the walk.

Travis grimaced. Chuck's snowmobile was parked on the front lawn. He must have come directly from the sheriff's office.

Warmth and the smell of stew met him when he entered. People filled the living and dining rooms, sitting or standing in small groups and speaking in low tones. Travis knew they were there to support Ellie, and he was glad for that, but the atmosphere was that of a funeral.

Ellie was in the dining room, her back to him, talking with Deputy Rogers and Chuck. Travis slipped off his boots, threw his jacket over the banister, and started toward Ellie.

An attractive middle-aged woman with heavily highlighted hair and a perfectly made-up face reached out a hand with rose-tinted nails and a huge diamond ring and laid it on his arm as he passed the overstuffed chair where she sat. He recognized her immediately. Mrs. Landry, wife of one of the wealthiest men in the area. Their mountain home was only one of three of their residences. He'd met her first at the boutique the day Dan was there. He'd met her since with her husband when they'd come in about a legal entanglement with a real estate purchase they planned to make.

"Good evening, Mrs. Landry."

She stood up. "My dear boy, I am so sorry about your little boy. I had to come over to tell Ellie my thoughts and prayers are with her and Corey. And you, too, of course."

"That's very kind."

"Ellie designs many of my clothes, you know."

He hadn't known, and though he knew it was a compliment to Ellie's talents, he didn't particularly care at the moment.

"That's how I know your son. He is the dearest boy."

Travis's impatience died an abrupt death. "Thank you. We think so."

"He and Jessica's little boy are such a cute twosome." She shook her head, making a *tsk-tsk-tsk-ing* sound Travis thought people made only in books. "So hard to believe all three of them are missing. I spoke with Jessica's husband Dan only yesterday."

"Yesterday? I thought he was out of town most of the day."

"I wouldn't know about that. I spoke to him in the morning. He's been preparing our tax returns—that is, my husband's and my personal tax return and my husband's business returns—for the last few years. We picked our returns up yesterday morning. I'm afraid we had to tell him he will no longer be our accountant." She laid a bejeweled hand on his arm again and leaned closer.

Travis instinctively reacted by leaning closer to her.

"It's his temper, you know." Her loud whisper wouldn't have required such close proximity. "We've no complaint with his professional abilities, but I don't trust a man with a temper like his. He created quite a scene at Ellie's boutique one day."

"Yes, I was there."

"So you were. I'd forgotten. Well, I told my husband about it, and he began asking about town, discreetly of course, concerning Dan's temper. My husband heard enough to convince him he no longer wants this man involved in any way with his business returns. He doesn't trust angry men. He says an angry man thinks with his emotions and not with his head."

Travis silently agreed. "Not a good plan for an accountant."

His dry humor appeared lost on Mrs. Landry, who only murmured a stammered, "N. . .no," and creased her perfectly made-up brow in a puzzled frown.

Travis politely excused himself and started toward Ellie once more. This time he was interrupted by Anna.

"Did you just arrive? You must be exhausted. There's hot stew in the kitchen. Are you hungry?"

Travis laughed and gave the woman a hug. "Yes, I just arrived. Yes, I'm exhausted. Yes, I'm hungry. The stew smells great. Did you make it?"

"One of the neighbors brought it in. I did make biscuits to have with it, though."

"I'll be in the kitchen for a bowl of stew and one of your biscuits after I say hello to Ellie." He glanced at her curiously. "Isn't that the same pants and top you were wearing when I left this morning?"

Her wrinkled cheeks flushed a pretty pink. "I didn't want to leave Ellie to go home and change."

"Have either of you slept at all?"

"I took a couple naps. Ellie laid down once or twice, but I don't think she slept. She took a shower a couple hours ago and said that refreshed her a bit. I think she's running on adrenaline, fear, and hope." She studied his face a moment. "Looks like you're doing the same."

"I think you're right. See you in the kitchen in a couple minutes."

He poked Ellie lightly on the shoulder with an index finger when he walked up behind her. She looked over her shoulder with only mild interest. When she recognized him her face lit up, lighting up his heart.

"You're back. Chuck said you were, but then. . ."

"I stopped for a shower and change of clothes. Wish I brought good news."

Her face fell into weary lines. "Deputy Rogers told me none of the search parties found any signs of Corey or the others."

Travis pushed her hair behind her ear with one hand. He could feel its dampness. She hadn't taken the time to dry or style it after the shower.

He wished they were alone. He wanted to pull her into his arms and pray together with her for their son. He wanted to tell her he loved her and he loved their son and what a terrible failure he felt as a father that he couldn't protect Corey from whatever it was that was happening to him. But he was afraid to do that would frighten her more. "How are you holding up?"

She nodded, closed her eyes a moment, and opened them again. "Fine."

It was a lie, of course. She wasn't doing fine. Neither was he. Admitting it in words might mean they would both break down. They couldn't afford to do that. What if Corey needed them and they weren't emotionally ready to help him?

"You should get some sleep. Anna and I will wake you if there's any news."

She hesitated, then nodded. "All right. I'll try. But you promise you'll wake me, no matter what the news?"

Even if it's the worst possible news. The words hung in the air between them.

He kissed her forehead, aching for her pain and fear, and for his own, and for their helplessness. "I promise."

"You need sleep, too."

"I'll lie down when you wake up. Right now I'm going to get something to eat."

As Travis headed for the kitchen, his gaze caught sight of the old print of a cabin on a snow-covered, wooded mountain hillside. It was a picture that kept recurring to him when he was out looking for Corey.

The picture had been interspersed with pictures of Corey and Brent: Brent pulling Corey on the sled, the boys helping him make the snowman, Corey dancing to a Barney song,

Corey pushing his way in between Travis and Ellie on the sofa, the boys drowning oyster crackers in bowls of tomato soup, their joy filling their faces and giggles filling the air.

He hoped they had something warm and nourishing to eat tonight. He hoped they were out of the cold, maybe in a place like that log cabin in the print. He hoped they were playing and giggling together. He hoped they hadn't been caught out in the storm. He hoped. . .

Change the picture, he demanded of his mind.

The one that replaced it wasn't a keeper: Chuck placing his hand against Ellie's cheek that morning, and Ellie covering the man's hand with her own. Travis wondered as he had so many times what Chuck meant to Ellie. He was pretty sure Chuck was sweet on her.

Travis remembered Ellie's kisses, the feel of her in his arms. Had it only been yesterday they'd embraced at the waterfall, that they'd laughed together running along the mountain path?

He hoped Ellie would decide to stay with him instead of choosing a life with Chuck or someone else, but whatever she decided, what he wanted most was her happiness. At least Travis was glad she was alive—she wasn't missing, maybe stranded on a mountain after a major snowstorm.

The thoughts had come full circle back to what he'd been trying to avoid, the thoughts that fatigued him to his very bones. *Keep Corey safe, Lord. Keep them all safe.*

Travis stopped, his hand on the swinging kitchen door.

A log cabin. That's what had been teasing at his fuzzy mind all day. The mountain cabin Dan and Jessica owned.

Would Jessica have taken the kids there? It was a long shot, but just maybe. . . .

His pulse raced. He turned and started running through the dining room. "Ellie!"

His shout stopped conversation. Everyone turned to watch him.

Ellie was in the living room, stopped by sympathetic friends before she could reach the stairway. She stared at him open-mouthed. "Corey? Is there news?"

He grabbed her hand. "No, sweetheart, no news. I just thought of something." He tugged her along with him toward the door, not bothering to apologize to their guests. "Get your coat. We're going to the sheriff's office."

She didn't protest or ask any more questions. She pushed her feet into boots and stuffed her arms into a red parka.

"What's going on?" Chuck stood with arms spread and a bewildered look on his tired face.

"Tell you later." Travis reached for Ellie's hand and they hurried out the door together.

The group Dan had searched with had just returned when Travis and Ellie arrived at the sheriff's office.

"Didn't find anything," the leader was telling Strand. He jerked a thumb at Dan and grinned. "Almost had to break off the search to go looking for this guy. He took a wrong turn in the woods."

Dan shrugged. "I would have realized my mistake before long."

Travis wondered. He'd seen for himself today how easy it would be to get lost in the thickly forested mountains.

Dan wiped a hand over wind-ruddied cheeks. "I was almost falling asleep out there."

Strand grunted. "Better go home and get some sleep."

"That's my plan. See you in the morning." The leader headed out. The rest of the search team followed. Dan was the last to head for the door.

"Wait a minute." Travis stopped Dan with a hand on his shoulder but spoke to the sheriff. "I finally figured out what's been nagging at me all day." He told them about the print of the log cabin.

Sheriff Strand rubbed a hand over his stubbly jaw and looked at Travis as if he'd lost his mind. "You're here about a painting?"

"Not exactly. The picture triggered a memory, a memory of

a mountain cabin Jess and Dan own."

Travis felt Dan's shoulder tense beneath his palm. "Where'd you hear about that?"

"Jess told me. A lawyer remembers things like shared assets when he's helping a woman with a divorce case." Was it his imagination or had Dan's eyes grown suddenly darker? The law firm he was with was big on watching body language. Sudden enlargement of pupils could denote fear or lying. Dan hadn't said anything that could be construed as a lie, had he? So what was he afraid of?

Strand beckoned Travis with a crook of his index finger. Travis followed him to a corner on the opposite side of the room from the sheriff's desk. "What's going on here, Carter? We don't have any reason to suspect Dan of foul play. His story of eating lunch with Jessica and the boys at the fast-food joint in Blowing Rock checked out. We had a copy of the photo you gave us and one of Dan sent over the wire and one of the workers at the restaurant remembered them. Right now you're as much a suspect as he is."

"I know all that." Travis was almost trembling from the energy racing through him. "I know the cabin is a long shot. We don't have any reason to believe Jess took the boys there. Maybe it's a coincidence that the picture of the cabin kept flashing in my mind all day while I was out searching. I can't explain it, but I have this urgent feeling that we should check that cabin out."

Sheriff Strand rubbed his jaw again. Travis could almost see Strand's tired mind going over the possibilities, weighing the chances of finding the three at a cabin against going home to a good night's sleep.

"Come on. The worst that can happen is that we eliminate one more possibility."

Strand heaved a huge sigh. "All right."

Back on the other side of the room Travis fought his impatience and waited for Strand to ask Dan the questions.

"About this cabin of yours, exactly where is it?"

Dan spread his arms and looked bewildered. "It's pretty remote. I can't imagine Jessie would go up there. She never liked the place. It's not some fancy vacation cabin. I use it mainly for hunting, let some of my cross-country skiing friends use it. Like I said, Jessie never liked the place."

"He's right." The look on Ellie's face told Travis she thought this was a wild goose chase.

"I still say we check it out." Travis held his breath, waiting for Strand to agree or nix the idea.

Dan's eyes sparked. "It's a waste of time, I tell ya."

"Don't you want to check out every possible lead in finding your son?" Travis made his voice as smooth as pudding.

"This isn't a lead. It's a fantasy. The best way I can help my son is to get a good night's sleep so I'll be fresh to go out with the search party again come dawn."

Strand walked over to a detailed map of the county that covered most of one wall of the office. "Where exactly did you say that cabin is located? Can you show me on this map?"

Dan made his way to the map wall, his boots clomping loudly on the linoleum-covered floor, his glance shooting daggers at Travis.

He studied the map for a minute, then jabbed an index finger at it. "There. That's where it is."

Strand shook his head. "You weren't kidding when you said it's a remote area. Is there even a road to that cabin of yours?"

"Only an old logging road. Not much more than a trail."

Strand stared at the map, considering.

If this idea about the cabin came from You, Lord, Travis prayed, *convince him to check it out.*

The sheriff turned and gave a stiff little nod. "All right, we'll see what's there."

"Yes." Travis lifted both fists in a triumphant gesture.

Immediately Sheriff Strand changed into a human efficiency machine. He ticked off what they'd need: a couple of four-wheel drives with trailers to carry snowmobiles, blankets, first-aid equipment, energy bars, and coffee. "We'll contact the

Highway Department and see if they can send up a plow if we decide we need one. And ask the hospital to have an ambulance standing by. I'll give Doc Abrams a call and see if he feels like making a house call. Ellie, you said Jessica and the boys were wearing spring clothes. Why don't you run home and get some warm things, just in case we have a break? Be back here in fifteen minutes."

Travis and Ellie made the trip in seventeen minutes. Sheriff Strand was ready to go when they arrived. A deputy Travis hadn't seen before was there, as was Doc Abrams. Travis nodded at them. "Thanks for coming."

"Yes, thank you." Ellie's smile made her face brighter than Travis had seen it since they'd discovered the boys were missing. Whether Jess and the boys were at the cabin or not, selecting warm clothes for them was good for Ellie's spirits. Travis knew it made her feel she was contributing something important to their rescue.

Dan, still scowling, was pacing the office.

"We want to go along." Travis wasn't about to take no for an answer. If nothing else, he'd follow in his Jeep uninvited. Strand would have to jail him to stop him.

"All right, but no back talk and no arguments."

"Done."

"You coming, too?" Strand slid into his jacket as he waited for Dan's answer.

"Yeah." He shuffled along behind the others toward the door.

Travis and Ellie were already outside when Travis heard Dan's wail.

"I can't. I can't do this. I can't do it."

Travis spun around, shock spiraling through him.

Ellie spoke sharply. "Get hold of yourself. If Brent is there, he might need you."

In the light from the office, Travis watched Dan's face crumple. Dan dropped his face into his hands. A keening split the night. He rocked back on his heels. "What have I done? Oh, what have I done?"

fourteen

Ellie stared at Dan, fear twisting through her, rooting her to the snow-covered ground. What was he talking about? Why was he making that high crying noise?

She dashed forward. Grabbed his hands. Pulled them from his face. "What are you talking about? Did you take Corey? Tell us." She shook his arms. "Tell us."

Travis's hands closed about her arms and pulled her back.

"Tell us."

Dan ignored her screaming demand and sunk to his knees on the ground just outside the door, rocking back and forth, continuing his keening.

Travis yanked him up by one arm. Dan hung from Travis's grip like a rag doll. "Where are the boys?"

"At the cabin. They're at the cabin."

Ellie could barely believe the words that jerked out between Dan's sobs.

"Are they all right? Have you hurt them?" Travis's voice sounded ragged, as if he'd torn the questions from his heart.

Ellie's strained to hear the answer.

"They. . .were. . .okay. . .when I. . .last. . .saw them."

Ellie dropped to the ground.

"Ellie." Travis was beside her instantly, his arms cradling her.

"I'm okay. I'm just so relieved." She giggled, feeling a bit hysterical. "My knees turned to mush."

Travis helped her up.

Sheriff Strand and his deputy had taken over when Travis dropped hold of Dan. They carried him inside and dropped him into a vinyl chair by Strand's desk. The others followed, Travis and Ellie last. Ellie's legs were still wobbly.

Someone brought Dan a cup of coffee.

Doc Abrams had other ideas. Ellie saw him pull a bottle

and a syringe from his bag. Was he planning to sedate Dan?

Evidently the sheriff thought the same thing. He held out a palm in a stop gesture. "Hold it. We need some more information here." His sharp tone held a note of something that sounded all too like anxiety to Ellie. "When did you leave them at the cabin, Dan?"

"Last night."

Ellie gasped, clasping her hands to her mouth. She'd been so relieved to hear Corey was all right when Dan last saw him that she hadn't thought how much time might have passed. Travis put his arms around her. She leaned into him, glad for his strength.

Sheriff Strand's face was grim while he pulled the information he needed from Dan. Dan continued his rocking motion throughout the questioning.

"Does Jessica have transportation?"

Dan shook his head.

"Why did she and the boys agree to go there with you?"

"I made them."

"How?"

"I had a gun."

Ellie groaned. She hid her face against Travis's shoulder to keep from crying out at the picture Dan created in her mind. Poor Corey. Poor Brent. They must have been so terrified.

"We don't have time for anything but the most important questions right now." Travis's words rasped above her ear. "Did you leave them food, Dan? Water? Firewood? Matches?"

Ellie felt the blood leave her face as all the possibilities were spoken.

"No food. But they'd just eaten. We went to the restaurant in Blowing Rock, remember?"

For lunch, Ellie recalled. That had been at least thirty hours ago. The boys would be hungry. They'd be crying.

A worse thought tightened her stomach. "Did you tell them you were coming back? What if they started walking and got caught in the storm?"

"They couldn't leave." Dan was rocking again, staring at

the floor. "The windows were boarded shut. Before I left, I nailed the door shut, too." He glanced up, searching the faces of the men standing about the room.

Ellie followed his gaze. Disgust and horror filled each face.

"I didn't plan it." Justification filled Dan's yelled words. "It was a spur-of-the-moment thing. I'd lost my most important client that morning, Landry. It was Jessie's fault. Landry's wife heard us fighting at the dress shop and decided I was unstable." He snorted. "I can tell you I handled Landry's tax returns quite competently for an unstable person. It's Jessie who's unstable. I was angry, and I went over to Jessie's. The hunting rifle was in the truck and. . .and the plan just popped into my mind, and I went with it."

"Let's go get the kids and Jess." Travis's tone said clearly that he had no more time for Dan.

Strand slapped a handcuff on one of Dan's wrists.

Dan cringed at the sight.

Strand cuffed the other hand. "You're coming with us. We don't want to miss that cabin. We want to find it on the first try."

Ellie and Travis followed the sheriff in Travis's Jeep. Every once in a while, Travis reached over and squeezed her hand. Most of the time he kept his attention on the road. They didn't say much to each other. A couple of times they prayed together. The rest of the time, prayers for Corey and Brent and Jessica's safety ran through Ellie's mind. She was sure they flashed through Travis's also.

The trip was a blur in Ellie's memory later. Travel was slow along the icy roads. The plow the sheriff had requested met them near the logging trail. Sheriff Strand, his deputy, and the doctor rode snowmobiles down the trail to the cabin. Ellie and Travis were left to follow the plow. Not even in the Jeep could Travis follow an unplowed logging trail through the woods at night after all the snow the storm had dropped.

When Ellie finally arrived at the cabin, the door had been removed. The boys and Jessica were wearing the clothes she'd sent ahead with the deputy. All three of them were seated on a hard bunk built into the wall, gulping down doughnuts.

"Corey." Ellie rushed to the bunk, feeling she couldn't get there fast enough. She wrapped her arms around him, burying her face in his neck. Tears ran down her cheeks.

"Oof." One of Corey's little palms pushed at her.

She loosened her hold only enough to see why he wanted out of her embrace. The half-eaten doughnut reminded her. With a laugh that was half sob, she released him.

Decided she couldn't stand it. Settling down on the bunk, she leaned back against the wall and hauled Corey onto her lap. He rested his back against her chest and kept eating. Satisfaction, contentment, and gratitude she hadn't known since the night he was born seeped through every cell of her body.

Ellie reached out a hand and ruffled Brent's hair. "Hi Brent."

He looked back at her with unsmiling eyes.

Her heart clenched. Brent and Corey had a lot of memories to undo. First thing tomorrow, she'd make an appointment for them with a counselor.

She met Jessica's gaze over Corey's head. For the first time she noticed her friend's black eye. Had she received it trying to protect herself and the boys from Dan? "Are you okay?"

Jessica nodded, touching a finger lightly to her bruise. "I was never so glad to have someone break down my door."

Ellie smiled gently. "Thank you for taking care of Corey."

"Any time. Did you and Travis have a nice picnic?"

Ellie heard Jessica's message loud and clear. They'd talk about the ordeal later out of the boys' hearing. Ellie smiled across the room at Travis. "I thought the picnic went well."

"Me, too." Travis's smile didn't quite reach his eyes. The expression in them was hungry as he watched Ellie and Corey.

Ellie's smile widened. "Why don't you come over and say hello?"

Travis crossed the small space in three slow steps, his gaze never leaving their son. He squatted beside the bunk. "Hi, partner."

Corey lifted a palm. "Hi, pa'dner."

"Hi, partner," Brent chimed in.

Travis grinned. "You two ready to go home?"

"Yes." Corey reached his arms toward Travis.

Travis hesitated. He glanced at Ellie.

Ellie nodded. Pure joy flooded her when Corey's arms hugged Travis's neck and Travis's eyes filled with tears.

Travis was almost at the door before Corey cried out, "Pony. Need Pony."

Ellie retrieved the gray horse from the bunk. Corey clutched it with a sigh of relief.

Ellie waited by the door for Jessica and Brent. The three of them walked out into the moonlit forest together.

ða

Ellie slept late the next morning, but as soon as her eyes opened she was wide awake. She stretched her arms toward the ceiling, unable to contain her joy. "Thank You, Lord."

She slipped out of bed and hurried into the boys' room. Both were still sleeping. She stood beside Corey's bed for a long time, absurdly happy just watching him breathe.

If Travis hadn't remembered the cabin Corey wouldn't be here now. She recalled the love and relief in Travis's eyes while he'd watched Corey at the cabin, the way Corey had reached for him, clung to him.

She'd clung to him, too, emotionally. What would she have done if he hadn't been with her through the ordeal? It seemed hard to believe she'd ever wondered whether she could trust him with Corey's love. She'd asked the Lord so many times whether Travis was trustworthy, or whether she was a fool to trust him with her and Corey's hearts. In every way Travis had acted lovingly and faithfully and trustworthily. After the last couple of days she couldn't imagine asking him to continue as a father who didn't share their lives in every way.

Her growling stomach reminded her she'd hardly eaten anything since she'd discovered Corey missing. Reluctantly she left Corey's bedside. She pulled on a sunny yellow sweater that matched her mood and comfortable jeans for a stay-at-home morning. She wouldn't bother to open the shop today.

She was breaking eggs for an omelette when Chuck arrived.

"I heard the good news. I had to stop and tell you how

happy I am for you."

"Thanks. And thank you for helping to search for them and for being here for me. You're a good friend."

He pulled his brown-and-blue corduroy baseball hat from his head and twirled it between his fingers. "Yeah, well. Guess you figured out I was hoping to be more than a friend one day."

Ellie wished he hadn't raised the subject. She hated coming right out and telling him again there was no place for him in her life as anything beyond a friend. "You're a good man. You'll make someone a—"

"Good husband one day," he finished with her.

They laughed together.

"About that husband of yours. . ."

"Yes?"

"I'm still not convinced that leopards change their spots. I don't know if you can trust him to be faithful to you. But I know he'd give his life to keep you and Corey safe, and that's not a small thing. If what you're looking for in a husband is a good father for Corey, you couldn't do better than the one he's already got."

"Thanks." Ellie knew how much it cost him to admit that. On impulse, she threw her arms around him. "Thanks for everything. You're the best."

He gave her a squeeze.

"Guess I came in at the wrong time."

Ellie started at Travis's unexpected voice. He was standing in the swinging doorway.

Chuck's arms fell away.

Ellie brushed a lock of hair behind her ear. "Travis. I wasn't expecting you."

"That's obvious. Don't let me interrupt." He turned on his heel. The door swung gaily in his wake.

Ellie turned pleading eyes on Chuck.

"Don't just stand there. Go after him."

It took a moment for his words to register. Then she grinned and gave him a silly little salute. "Aye, aye, sir."

He returned the salute and stepped out the back door as she rushed into the hallway.

She reached Travis on the front porch and grabbed his arm. "Don't go. Please. We have to talk."

He didn't look as if he wanted to talk, but he allowed her to lead him back into the house and into the living room. They faced each other in the middle of the room.

"Travis, I—"

"You don't have to apologize."

"But I—"

"Let me finish. This isn't easy to say."

She pressed her lips together to keep back the words of love she wanted to shout.

He took a deep breath. "These last couple days not knowing whether Corey was alive or dead taught me a lot. I learned what Anna tried to tell me."

"About what?"

"She asked me how much I loved you and Corey, whether I loved you enough to want what was best for you even if that meant I didn't share your lives. I've tried to love you that way. After this weekend I think I finally understand what she meant, understand it in my heart, not only my head. I want us to live together under one roof as a family in every sense of the word. But more than that I want you to both be healthy and safe and happy. I never want to go through another sixty seconds of the kind of fear I felt this weekend. I don't know how to make you trust me as a husband and father. I can only leave you in God's hands. I know you'll try to follow God's leading in your life. Whatever your decision is about us, I'll respect it, even if you choose to marry Chuck."

She shook her head, smiling softly. "I have no romantic interest in Chuck."

Travis jerked his gaze to the ceiling and snorted. "Right. I saw the evidence for myself. You were in his arms not five minutes ago."

"Well, yes, but—"

"I heard you tell him. . .you told him he's the best."

She heard the pain in his voice. "It wasn't the way you think." A memory popped into her mind, a memory of herself saying, "I heard you; I saw you." She pressed her fingertips to her lips to suppress a laugh.

"What's so funny?"

"You're the lawyer. Evidence isn't always what it seems, is it?"

"Not always, but when there's an eyewitness—"

"Like I was an eyewitness to Michelle returning your cuff links and saying you'd left them in her apartment?"

He swung an arm toward the kitchen. "It's not the same thing. I saw. . .I heard. . ." His arm fell. He stared at her. "Wow. So that's what it was like for you." He wiped a hand over his face. "No wonder you left. No wonder you find it so hard to trust me. When I saw you and Chuck. . .it hurt so much I thought I couldn't bear it. And then when I thought you were lying to me about caring for him. . ."

Ellie's throat constricted painfully. "Yes, that's what it was like."

His hands enveloped hers. "I promise what I told you about that night at Michelle's is true. She was never more than a friend to me. I've never been unfaithful to you."

She looked down at their joined hands. All the fears she'd nursed so attentively the last three years filled her mind and twisted her stomach. What if he was lying? What if she opened her heart to him completely and he betrayed her? But there was no way to guarantee another person's love and faithfulness. Only God's love came with a guarantee. Trusting anyone was a choice, a calculated risk. Travis's actions the last few months seemed those of a faithful, loving man, she reminded her fears. How long and in how many ways did she expect him to prove himself before she gave him her trust?

She made her choice. She took a deep shaky breath and looked into his eyes. "I believe you. What I told you about Chuck is true, too. He's only a friend. Believe me?"

He nodded. He lifted a hand to cup her cheek, caressing her face gently with his thumb. "It must have taken so much trust in God and so much Christ-like love for me for you to tell me about Corey. You had so little reason to trust me then. You still believed I'd been unfaithful. You didn't even know I'd come to believe in God."

"Corey is your son. You had a right to know him."

"I'm sorry about the whole Michelle incident."

"Don't." Ellie pressed fingers to his lips. "Don't speak about it again. It's behind us. I shouldn't have run out on you that way. I should have given you a chance to explain. I wanted to protect myself from any more emotional pain more than I wanted to stay faithful to the 'us' that is you and me. I guess there's more than one way to be unfaithful in a marriage. By not giving you a chance to explain, I was unfaithful to you. I'm sorry."

He kissed the fingers that were still at his lips, sending tingles along her nerves. "Like you said, it's behind us. I believe God meant for us to stay together as a family instead of separate the way we did, but God never wastes any experience. He's used our time apart to bring each of us to faith in Him and to teach us more about love."

"Yes." There was no doubt left in her heart as to what she wanted with this man, but she trembled inside at the risk. Living together as husband and wife would make her so vulnerable again. Was that life's next lesson, staying vulnerable to those she loved?

She took a shaky breath. "If you don't mind, I'd like us to learn the rest of God's lessons together, as husband and wife and as Corey's parents. That is, if you still want us to be a family."

The joy in his eyes told her everything she needed to know, but he answered anyway. "If I still want us to be a family?"

He caught her in his arms, lifting her from her feet and swinging her around in a circle. When he stopped, his kisses started. Gently he touched his lips to her temple, her eyebrow, her eyelid, her cheek, making a trail to her lips.

"Any doubts left about whether I still want us to be a family?"

She smiled against his lips.

He led her to the sofa and pulled her back into his arms on the comfy cushions. "Let's talk about our plans."

"What do we need to talk about?"

"Where we'll live, for starters."

"Don't you want to live here?"

"It's a great house, but do we plan to keep living with Jess and Brent?"

"I hadn't thought about it. I guess getting back together isn't going to be as simple as I thought."

Travis chuckled. "I think we'll be able to work it out if we keep our heads together."

For the next few minutes they sat quietly, content to hold each other and bask in the joy of rediscovered love.

Ellie stirred slightly. "Next Sunday is Easter."

"Mmmm. So it is. We have a lot to be thankful for this Easter."

"Will you go to church with me and Corey?"

"We've never gone to church together, except for our wedding. What a great way to begin our new life together."

"There's something we need to do first."

"What's that?"

"Introduce Corey to his father."

He didn't respond.

Ellie pulled her head from his shoulder to look at him. Tears glistened in his eyes.

"You sure Corey will want me as his father?"

She pictured the way Corey had reached for him at the cabin. A slow grin spread across her face. "I'm sure."

❧

With the inconsistency of spring weather in the Carolina mountains, Easter was sunny and warm. The little snow that had survived the week since the storm ran in cheerful rivulets down the village's hillside sidewalks and streets. Birds sang their songs and searched for food in the grass sticking through the last of the snow.

Inside the stone church, the sun's rays fell warmly through

the stained-glass windows. Music rejoicing in God's gift of His Son swelled, filling the sanctuary to the rafters.

Travis looked down at Corey. The boy sat between Travis and Ellie in a sharp little blue suit Ellie had designed for him. His pointed chin rested on the gray pony he clutched to his chest.

Travis felt as if his heart would explode from ecstacy. At Christmas he hadn't known if he'd ever have a chance to meet Corey. *Thank You, Father, that I won't be spending Corey's first thirty-three years apart from him. Thank You for sending Your own Son, Jesus, to show us the way of love.*

Ellie's gaze met Travis's above Corey's golden curls. She smiled, and Travis felt wrapped in her love.

Together the three of them waited patiently after the service in the line to shake Pastor Evanson's hand, with Corey in Travis's arms. They visited with friends and neighbors, acknowledging the many who expressed their thanksgiving that Corey, Brent, and Jessica were safe.

Sunshine warmed them as they stepped through the large wooden doors onto the church's front steps. Ellie took the pastor's hand. "Thank you for all the prayer support you gave us last week."

"Yes, thank you." Travis grasped the man's hand warmly.

Corey stuck out one little hand.

Pastor Evanson took it with a laugh.

Corey pointed at Ellie. "That's Mom." He shoved an index finger against Travis's white shirt. "This is my dad. We're a fambly."

"So you are." The pastor grinned.

Ellie gave Travis a flirtatious grin that made his heart jump. "So we are."

Travis held Corey securely with one arm. He slid the other around Ellie's waist and smiled down at her as they started down the stone steps. "Amen."

A Letter To Our Readers

Dear Reader:

In order that we might better contribute to your reading enjoyment, we would appreciate your taking a few minutes to respond to the following questions. We welcome your comments and read each form and letter we receive. When completed, please return to the following:

Rebecca Germany, Fiction Editor
Heartsong Presents
PO Box 719
Uhrichsville, Ohio 44683

1. Did you enjoy reading *Come Home to My Heart?*
   ☐ Very much. I would like to see more books
   by this author!
   ☐ Moderately
   I would have enjoyed it more if _____
   _____
   _____

2. Are you a member of **Heartsong Presents**? Yes ☐ No ☐
   If no, where did you purchase this book?_____
   _____

3. How would you rate, on a scale from 1 (poor) to 5 (superior), the cover design?_____

4. On a scale from 1 (poor) to 10 (superior), please rate the following elements.

   _____ Heroine   _____ Plot

   _____ Hero   _____ Inspirational theme

   _____ Setting   _____ Secondary characters

se characters were special because_____

_____

_____

6. How has this book inspired your life?_____

_____

_____

7. What settings would you like to see covered in future
   Heartsong Presents books?_____

_____

_____

8. What are some inspirational themes you would like to see
   treated in future books?_____

_____

_____

9. Would you be interested in reading other **Heartsong
   Presents** titles?   Yes ❏   No ❏

10. Please check your age range:
    ❏ Under 18   ❏ 18-24   ❏ 25-34
    ❏ 35-45   ❏ 46-55   ❏ Over 55

11. How many hours per week do you read?_____

Name _____

Occupation _____

Address _____

City _____ State _____ Zip _____